ETERNAL

DAMNATION

ETERNAL

DAMNATION

STORIES

Eric Larsen

atmosphere press

for

Debra Poulter

and

Anthony Stonier—

for keeping our spirit alive

The past was dead, the future was unimaginable. What certainty had he that a single human creature now living was on his side?

—George Orwell, 1984

Table of Contents

1

1

Eternal Damnation

No one in my family really believed in god anymore, but none of them would admit it, at least not in so many words, not even my father. And so, for a handful of years following 1947, the year we moved out of town and to the farm, we still made a pious show of driving back into town and attending church. My parents and older sister would go to the regular service, while my younger sister and I disappeared into the mildewy basement for "Sunday school."

I hated going. This was especially true during nice weather. I was seven or eight, the youngest in the family and the first to get up each morning. Church was at eleven, and by then I'd already have been up for hours. Having to take off my soft and familiar "everyday" clothes and change into the stiff, sharp-edged ones was an agony that made me think of pulling on cold sheets of tin.

One warm and perfect fall afternoon as we were coming home from church, I saw Charlie Engle out in Murray Wither's pasture across the road from our house, batting a ball into the air and catching it as it came down. I knew this meant a game was coming together. Upstairs, I tore off my church clothes and jumped back into my soft and worn ones, grabbed my bat from behind the kitchen door, took my mitt off its peg, and ran across the road into the pasture.

There were ten all together and we played until the end of the afternoon. I got along with everyone except Charlie's oldest sibling, his brother Bill. Bill was sixteen and a bully. He resented me and my family because we'd moved out of town to the farm instead of having been born and raised out in the country like his own family and all the others. He was also big for his age, not fat, but heavy and muscular. All afternoon it was necessary for me to endure him. When the teams switched for new innings, he made sure to saunter nearby and give me a punch on the shoulder, hard enough to hurt. If I said anything about it he'd make a show of crying like a baby. He was supposed to play positions both at shortstop and second base. As the game went on he took pleasure in making loud remarks, baiting me about my sisters and making gross, suggestive taunts about them.

In the end, it was as if some kind of divine force guided me. On the last play, Jerry Winter threw a weak but perfect pitch, and I swung at it with every fiber of muscle I had. Bill wasn't paying attention, and the ball flew in a line drive to slap against his left temple with a sound like an oiled blackjack. He actually went down for a second, and he swung his head like a dazed bull before he looked over to home base, where I remained standing, as still as a stump but with a grin on my face as big as a split melon. His outrage was instantaneous, and he came for me. But I was already well away from home base and halfway to the road before he was even up on his feet.

Sprinting with delight toward our farmhouse, I reveled in the blow I had delivered and in the wonderful justice of it. Only later, at suppertime, when one of my sisters bowed her head to murmur grace, did I remember what day it was, and the church basement, and my hated Sunday clothes. It occurred to me then that what I had done might have been a sin, and that I might face eternal damnation and agony unending for it. But the satisfaction was too great, and by the time supper was over I had cast that doubt from my mind.

5

2

Whiteout

(1954-2001)

An afternoon in mid-March of 1953 brought my first memorable reference to the calamitous ruin that would cripple the nation half a century later.

Storm-forecasting at that time was not so unrelentingly sophisticated as now, and there was less interest in stirring up fear in regard to "threatening events."

A storm could come up with too little warning for the weather forecasters to predict its severity. They were less able to scare people into making cancelations and the like before a storm arrived rather than after it had begun.

When I left the farmhouse that morning with my sisters to walk out and wait for the school bus at the edge of the road, everything seemed routine. The sky was low and gray, the air calm, faintly moist, at a temperature somewhere near the freezing point. But after ten o'clock, snow began to fall outside the schoolroom windows, tiny flakes at first, though steady. As time went on the snowfall became thicker, and by the time we went down into the basement for lunch, a wind had come up and you could see it worrying the snow—sweeping and whirling it across the bare dirt of the playground.

In short, the snowfall grew heavier and the wind stronger. Drifts began to form on the lee sides of structures and objects, including the wooden fence around the playground.

At one o'clock the principal sent staff members from room to room to announce that school was to be closed early. Bus drivers were being alerted to come for pickup as quickly as possible.

Of course things took much longer than expected. Students who lived in town simply walked home along their usual routes, shuffling through the deepening snow. But for those who lived out in the country, it was another matter. Many of the school bus drivers had jobs other than driving, and they had to be summoned from the locations of those jobs, make their way back to the bus garage, and from there drive to whichever school was their first pickup—all the while contending with the increasingly poor visibility and the drifting snow. One bus went off the road and had to be towed back on. The first bus to reach our own school didn't arrive until near three o'clock, almost the regular closing time.

Then, too, just driving the regular homebound routes took longer than normal. My own bus never did make it to the end of its route, since the driver, like a number of others, decided it would be safer to let his last few passengers off at the bus garage, so that from there they could hitch rides in the cars of whatever homebound drivers might be going in their direction.

That's how I came to be in Kester Frandrup's car that afternoon, sometime after four o'clock. Kester lived on a farm four miles or so northwest of the bus garage, near a crossroads town named Elko. My own family lived just a mile or so from the bus garage, in the same direction as Elko. Kester could easily drop me off on his way past.

Also in the car were Art Prior and his brother Dave, whose

family lived another half mile down the road from mine. Art was two years ahead of me, Dave a year behind. Also in the car was Sandy Kucera, a seventh grader like me, whose family lived another mile closer to Elko.

The four of us waited inside the garage while Kester drove his bus out to its usual parking place at the rear of the lot. This took some time because the empty spaces had drifted in, and George Paisley, the garage owner, mechanic, and manager, had to get up on his tractor with the snowblade hooked onto it and plow the stalls out before the last of the buses could pull in.

I didn't know where Kester had parked his car, but Art Prior had been looking out through a window in one of the rear doors and, after a long wait, said,

"Here he comes. He'll be up at the front."

The wind was strong. It whistled around the corners of the garage and drove lines of snow through those places where the windows weren't snug. When gusts hit against the roof just so, they made booming sounds in the cavernous interior.

The enormous front door was hung on rollers so it could be pushed aside for bringing in buses and other large equipment, but off to one side of it a smaller door of regular size had been cut for people to go in and out even when the big door was closed. When Art opened the little door, it swung inward with a powerful snap and snow blew in, stinging against your face. We plodded single file to the car and Dave got into the back, followed by Sandy and then me. Art got in front beside Kester and pulled the door shut. For a second or two things felt cozy and safe. Kester put the car in gear and we crept away from the garage toward the edge of the highway. The snow was blowing thickly enough so that some of the time all you could see was white outside the windows. Kester waited at the edge of the highway, not moving, until a break came and he could see at least a little distance up the way. When it seemed fairly certain that nothing was coming, he let out the clutch and we went across.

As I said, this happened in 1953, when I was twelve years old and in seventh grade. As usual when finding myself in the company of a grown man whom I didn't know, I felt unsure of myself and slightly afraid because of being accustomed to my own father's sullenness, unpredictability, and quickness to anger. But Kester was different. He was casual and easy-going and talked with us the way he might have talked with anyone else. He even got us to help out. At the edge of the highway, he asked Art to look off to the right for cars, and Dave to the left. Once we were across the highway and onto the gravel road going west, we settled into a steady pace, mostly in second gear, sometimes even in first, through the drifts. This part of the trip was when Kester said the thing I remembered for six decades.

"Well," he said, "this is one sure good night for keeping your feet by the fire and your head by the television set."

I said nothing, but his remark struck me as chill, strange, and alien. My own family didn't have a television set, although the Priors did—a small-screened, flickering, snow-filled thing that I'd once watched a cowboy rodeo on. Neither the television nor the experience of watching it had any connotation for me of coziness, contentedness, security, or warmth. They must have had those things for Kester, though, and for millions of others.

•

Fifty years later, in 2004, I was coming close to retirement from the faculty position I'd held for the past third of a century. During those decades of teaching, I often wrote book reviews and sometimes other short pieces on the subjects of books and reading.

This is one of them, a revisiting of Hans Zinsser's *Rats, Lice and History*, a book published all the way back in 1935. I include it here because when I wrote its closing line, I was thinking of the day in 1954 when the blizzard came, when school was closed, and when I got a ride home in Kester Frandrup's car—when I heard the first hint of the catastrophe that was to become inevitable when reading ended and television took over. Television would pander to the population with its trillions of small betrayals that would make the catastrophic betrayal, in September of 2001, invisible to everyone who saw it. Even though they saw it with their own eyes. Or with what had once been their own eyes.

•

Two-thirds of a century ago, Hans Zinnser published *Rats, Lice and History*, still in print today. The book is a "biography" of typhus, and Zinsser says he wrote it "at odd moments as a relaxation from studies of typhus fever in the laboratory and in the field." Maybe those "odd moments" are what made the book so pleasantly rambling and discursive: reading it today can make you feel you're actually back there, in 1935, in a comfortable room with this affable and well-educated host who knows everything and also loves to talk about it.

Zinsser's learning is impressive, albeit worn lightly. He roams from antiquity to the present, is equally knowledgeable about ancient literary figures (Herodotus, Homer, the rest) as about contemporary (Irving Babbitt to Ezra Pound, Laurence Sterne to Gertrude Stein), and is at home with handfuls of languages, classic Greek among them—all the while telling the twin tale of typhus on the one hand and the fate of nations on the other, making it clear that germs are the giants of history, and "that soldiers have rarely won wars." Instead, "They more often mop up after the barrage of epidemics."

Scientific objectivity can make for an amusingly

sassy irreverence, as when Zinsser points out that in early Christianity, "every great calamity—famine, earthquake, and plague—led to mass conversions, another indirect influence by which epidemic diseases contributed to the destruction of classical civilization." Thus: "Christianity owes a formidable debt to bubonic plague and to smallpox, no less than to earthquake and volcanic eruptions."

Skeptical, perhaps, but nothing if not humane, and Zinsser's humanity found its expression in a time that now seems very far back indeed. The author is appalled by the catastrophe that was WWI, and he has no inkling of the even greater catastrophe so soon to follow. "It can well be said that nobody won the last war except the medical sciences. The profit was not worth the loss, but the increase in sanitary and medical knowledge was the sole determinable gain for mankind in an otherwise utterly disastrous catastrophe."

What would he think of the world now, all these years and wars later?

Even on the subject of reading and writing his voice is comforting. "Writing," he says, "like speech, is a...means of conveying to others emotions, conceptions, or original comprehensions which might instruct, amuse, or elevate." At one time, reading was only for the elite. "In our day, however, all kinds of people can read: college professors and scrubwomen, doctors and lawyers, bartenders, ministers of the gospel and trained nurses. They all have the same ideal of the happy ending of a dull day—a comfortable couch, a bed lamp, and something to read."

Ah, the past! Ah, the ideal! Zinsser's life ended in 1940, just a decade or so before television came, and the reading lamps went out all over America.

2

1

Transit

One afternoon in autumn 1912, on her uncle's farm in Minnesota, she sat on the lawn and watched an apple tree fill up with Monarch butterflies. As she sat there, more and more butterflies flew up and landed until the tree seemed to be made up not of branches and leaves at all but only of quietly fanning, brilliant wings.

Sunshine flooding down from a blue sky added brightness to the sight.

The girl's name was Hannah and she was not yet five years old. But she was to remember this afternoon and the tree of butterflies for the rest of her life—a life that, as she approached its end, seemed to her to have been hardly more than a few moments long.

2

The Past

From time to time I think of people whose lives took place long ago.

I turned eighty-three a few months ago, and one of the people I thought of then was Alice J., who visited me in a distant memory. Alice J.—she was known almost universally by that name—was my mother's mother's mother, and near the end of her life she lived in a suite of three rooms plus bath over Schilling's Feed and Supply Store, on Fifth Street and Main.

The only way up to the floor she lived on was by an external staircase bolted onto the side of the building, with iron struts angled underneath to give it strength. The staircase railing was spindly, and the steps themselves had no risers, so that a child felt certain of falling through the back of each step or of being sucked out into thin air.

The memory I had recently was from April of 1944, the month I turned four. I was certain we were all—my mother, brother, sister, and I—going to fall or be swept to our deaths as we waited on the tiny platform at the unspeakable height of the stair-top for Alice J. to open the door into the dark hallway that would lead to her own door at the far end. Her sitting room was small and dim and had old-fashioned furniture and old-fashioned lighting. Alice J. herself was eighty-four years old at the time and, like many old people, she was sweetly solicitous of children and made every effort to please them. We were all sitting down, I remember, when she leaned forward in her own chair and said to me and my siblings, "You children will live to see the end of the millennium. But I won't. I won't be here any more by then." Soon after, she stood and picked up a silver candy dish from a side table, then stepped over to the horsehair loveseat where my siblings and I sat in a row, elbow to elbow. Alice J. came to me first because I was on the closer end. She leaned forward and in the same movement lifted the lid to offer a piece of the candy inside. The dish held maple-sugar sweets pressed into the shape of pine trees. But I didn't take one because the candies were obscured by a thick moving blanket of ants.

The past. Symbols lie nestled in these bits of memory from nearly a century ago—more than I have mentioned—and they remain capable of moving me greatly. But I see no point in writing them down, since the world, as I have watched it change around me, especially of late, no longer shows the least understanding of the past or cares about it in any way whatsoever.

3

The Girl from Ancient Pages

The space between outer and inner doors was small—a vestibule—and I was surprised to find a tall young woman there as I came in from the street, my key at the ready. She was leaning in a casually slumped sort of way against one of the closet-like walls.

"Hello," I said.

"Hello," she replied as, standing up straight, she took a step toward me, one hand out, palm up. There lay a key ring, and on it three keys of shiny new brass. She held them out to my view.

"Could you help me?" she asked, and then, without pause, waiting for no response from me, she went on: "I don't live in this building, but I've come to stay with my aunt. She gave me these keys to use while I'm here, but I wonder if they're right. I can't seem to unlock the front door."

Her voice was soft, whispery, delicate, and precise. In every way it was pleasant.

"Could I give it a try?" I asked.

I took the ring, selected the front door key, and inserted it into the lock. Exactly like my own, it refused to turn at first, seeming to hit against some kind of a block inside. But after I wriggled it quickly a time or two, the way I would with my own key, it meshed with the pins and the lock opened.

"Oh," said the young woman.

"My key is like that too," I said, "almost always." I held the door open. The young woman stepped in and I followed. I gave the keys back to her.

"You have to wriggle it a bit," I said.

"Oh. Wriggle it. I see," she replied. "I'm so grateful. I thought I would never get in."

We walked together across the lobby. The lobby was cool, quiet, and empty. No one was sitting behind the concierge's desk. As the girl walked beside me, I realized that she was not just tall but very tall. She and I stood facing the elevator. The red LED light over the door showed that the car was on the fifteenth floor and descending.

"So where are you arriving from?" I asked the young woman.

"I'm returning from Italy," she answered. "I've been there for the past two years."

"Oh. I see."

The car arrived, the door slid silently open, and we stepped in.

"Which floor?" I asked.

"Fourteen, please."

I pushed fourteen and then seven. "I'm halfway up to you," I said foolishly.

The young woman laughed lightly. "Yes," she said. Then, as the elevator began going up, a number of things happened, almost all at once. For one, I realized that her height made her at least a head taller than me, so that I craned upward just to see her face. She leaned against the side of the car in the same way she had leaned against the wall of the vestibule—with poor posture, one hip higher than the other, one arm bent at the elbow, suspended from it a shopping bag, the other arm hanging down limply, like a rope with no weight on it. Her long neck was angled slightly forward, in an almost-graceful bird-like way. On the whole, she seemed to be constructed of all kinds of angles at odds with one another, each pointing in a different direction from the others—and yet at the same time she was quite, quite beautiful. Her auburn hair was abundant, most of it drawn up onto the crown of her head, with the rest managing to cascade across her shoulders. As for her face, it, too, seemed made of contrasting angles—strong chin, thin and slightly aquiline nose, high cheekbones, large eyes set under slightly hooded brows, unusually high forehead— and yet the oddly dissimilar elements of her face fell into a unity that produced a breath-taking effect. The young woman was in no sense pretty. But she was sweepingly beautiful.

And then, above all else, there was her voice: soft and delicate yet firm and precisely delivered. It evoked the passing of a breeze through summer foliage, or a gentle wind crossing a field of standing wheat. I could—I was certain—have listened to her voice forever.

I stepped slightly closer to her, away from the very old elevator operator in his brass-buttoned uniform, and asked, "And where were you in Italy?"

But she misunderstood me. Instead of identifying where she'd been, she answered, "I was there on a fellowship." Then, exactly as she had done in the vestibule, she followed up with a flood—a quiet, melodic, pleasing flood—of attendant but wholly unsolicited information. "You see, my family comes from St. Louis, where my sister and I both grew up, and where our aunt also lived, until 1911, that is, when she came here to New York. You can understand why I don't want to return to St. Louis. Not after having lived where I've been living and doing what I've been doing there...."

At that moment the elevator glided silently to a stop, and

the wizened operator said,

"Seventh floor."

He drew back the long lever his hand rested on and the gate, with a quiet and well-oiled swooshing sound, folded itself to one side, offering open passage onto the seventh floor. I stepped out, but as I did so I glanced back at the young woman. Our eyes met, and I saw that she was smiling slightly.

I stood looking into the interior of the car as the gate once more swept closed.

"Well," I said through the interstices of the closed gate, "I wish you the very best of luck."

"Thank you," she replied in the voice that seemed to hold within it sunlight, soft breezes, the sighing of Renaissance angels. The elevator rose. The young woman's face, shoulders, arms rose up and disappeared from my view; then went the remainder of her silken dress, ivory-white, its hem all but touching the floor of the car.

Since then, I have thought a thousand times of this tall and beautiful young woman, have imagined what it would be like if our paths were to cross, have yearned to meet her again and listen to her extraordinary voice, study her character, sample the immensities of meaning that must have been held within her.

In the many decades since then, however, I have never seen her again.

3

1

A Perfect Morning

Lies are truth. Sickness is health. Fraud is candor.

Madness is sanity.

Such words and phrases were going through his head as he took the elevator down, passed through the foyer, then went out the front entrance of the building onto the sidewalk.

The morning was beautiful. The sky was clear and actually blue for once, not covered by the usual steel-gray haze that made it look as if skim milk had been poured into it. The air was fresh and pleasantly cool against his skin.

He walked down to the corner, where greetings came from the Yemini guys sitting outside their housewares store. The same came from Manuel at the flower stand. Manuel's cat, when he bent down to scratch her ears, rolled onto her back to welcome a belly rub.

He walked to the end of the block and got a large coffee from Lenny's Bagel Shop. Then he returned the way he had come, carrying the coffee past the cat, past Manuel, and past the Yeminis at their store.

When he was in his apartment again, in the front room, at

his desk, coffee near at hand, he opened his computer, drew its keypad toward him, and typed two sentences:

"Today is May 20th, 2021. Our 'leaders' want all of us dead as soon as possible."

2

My Last Years

i

It is Thursday, September 22nd, 2022. Summer will end today and autumn begin. I look it up and find that the equinox will take place at 9:03 p.m. That means there are six or seven hours of summer left to go, since this indolent, lazy, blue-skied day is now entering mid-afternoon. Thirteen minutes past two, the clock says. Even though these are the last few hours of summer, the day already feels like true autumn. Warm, hushed, still. The afternoon air, when tufts of it glide gently in through my open window, is fragrant in at least one or two dozen of the thousand soft and melancholy ways autumn air can be fragrant. Unlike any of the other seasons, as everyone knows, autumn has the ability, at any moment, to sweep a person back through time. It happens that way for me now. After a sweet draft of air from the window, I am no longer at my desk, no longer in the front room of my apartment, no longer in New York City, and neither on the West Side nor looking down on a sleepy 99th Street. Instead, I am transported

27

seven decades into the past. Seventy years have collapsed into nothing. I'm no longer a retiree about to turn eighty-one, but instead (living in distant memory) I'm a kid a month or two away from his eleventh birthday, and I have just completed the first two weeks or so of sixth grade.

Dismissal time was three o'clock in the afternoon. Going downstairs and passing out through the front entrance was like emerging into heaven, into a world of sweetness, stillness, sunshine, scent, warmth.

The memory is powerful but also short-lived. In an instant I'm at my desk again, gazing down on 99th Street, watching a young woman walk toward West End Avenue holding the hands of two children. The woman is wearing a red dress. I try to guess the ages of the children, a girl and a boy. The girl is a head taller than the boy, whom I suppose to be, though I will never know, her brother.

When the three reach West End Avenue, they turn to the right, uptown, and in an instant they have disappeared around the corner. I feel with a sudden and powerful although dreadful and emotionless certainty that I will never see them again, no matter how much longer my own life may go on.

When I turn back to my desk and open the file that I've named "Literary Club," my attention is caught yet again by this short piece, entitled "A Perfect Morning." I feel as though I must have written it just a day or two ago, although it's already well over a year old:

> *Lies are truth. Sickness is health. Fraud is candor.*
>
> *Madness is sanity.*
>
> *Such words and phrases were going through his head as he took the elevator down, passed through the foyer, then went out the front entrance of the building onto the sidewalk.*
>
> *The morning was beautiful. The sky was clear and actually blue for once, not covered by the usual steel-gray haze that made it look as if skim milk had been poured into it. The air was fresh and pleasantly*

cool against his skin.

He walked down to the corner, where greetings came from the Yemini guys sitting outside their housewares store. The same came from Manuel at the flower stand. Manuel's cat, when he bent down to scratch her ears, rolled onto her back to welcome a belly rub.

He walked to the end of the block and got a large coffee from Lenny's Bagel Shop. Then he returned the way he had come, carrying the coffee past the cat, past Manuel, and past the Yeminis at their store.

When he was in his apartment again, in the front room, at his desk, coffee near at hand, he opened his computer, drew its keypad toward him, and typed two sentences:

"Today is May 20th, 2021. Our 'leaders' want all of us dead as soon as possible."

ii

Our literary club meets once a week, on Mondays, invariably at five o'clock, since that's the hour when our meeting place, the Italian bar and restaurant called "Regional," opens for business. I and a very small group of friends—there are four of us—exchange pieces of our own writing, poems, stories or other prose, then analyze and discuss them. Just as often, we decide on a piece of real literature to read and discuss. Most of the time these choices come from among the "classics" that I covered in my decades of teaching. We've read Aeschylus, Sophocles, and Euripides, Shakespeare (some), *Great Expectations*, *To the Lighthouse*, *Waiting for Godot*, others. I look forward to these meetings and enjoy them tremendously, in fact increasingly so as my despair deepens.

As for how old the woman in the red dress may have been, I imagine her as being somewhere in her middle thirties. As for the children—I use the memory of my own children for measurement—I imagine the daughter as having been seven years old, perhaps eight, since she stood a head taller than her little brother, whom I think of as being five.

My absolute certainty that I will never see them again is fallacious, of course. It isn't possible to *know* that I won't see them. Or, for that matter, it's possible that I might see them and not even know it. After all, I didn't see the young woman's face and so I couldn't recognize her by facial appearance. As for the red dress, she might never wear it again. There was no way, really, I'd be aware it was the same woman unless I saw her again, with two children, in the red dress, on 99th Street, disappearing around the corner.

•

In 1952, the 22nd of September fell on a Monday. At the Longfellow School, there were two sections of sixth grade, and mine was taught by a young woman we knew by her last name only, addressing her as Miss Stryk. The name was pronounced exactly as it is in the phrase "strike up the band."

At the time, Miss Stryk seemed to me at least as old as my parents. I'm certain now, however, that she must even then have been a decade younger than the woman in the red dress who was walking with her children on 99th Street.

I'm all but certain I will never see Miss Stryk again in what may remain of my life—or of hers, if any remains of that. But the young woman in the red dress is another matter. People are disappearing. The crowds on Broadway—whether in the morning, at midday, or in the evening—have never come back to what they were before March of 2020, when the world began ending—or, more accurately, when the world began being brought to an end by malevolent, insane, unelected cowards. I doubt now that the crowds will ever come back to what they were. When we have our literary club we're sometimes the only ones in the restaurant. People are disappearing rather than returning. I fear that the young woman in the red dress may also go away, may stop being. I have seen her only once, and I will probably never see her again. I wish this were not so. I don't need her as a friend. But even so, I wish—powerfully—that she would not disappear, like the others.

31

3

Death

In my last year at Longfellow Elementary School, as I mentioned earlier, there were two sections of sixth grade. Going into seventh grade marked an enormous change, since it meant moving across the river to the east side of town and having classes in the ancient old building named after no legislator or poet but called simply "West Tree Junior-Senior High School."

Things felt very grown up there. Not only did each student have his or her own locker out in the hallway, but each class met in a different room for each class-hour of the day and also had a different teacher for each.

The building dated from 1890, although there was a modern addition attached to its north flank that had been built in 1933. I very much preferred the old part. There, the ceilings in the hallways loomed high overhead, and even the locker that was assigned to me seemed immense. The classrooms were also high-ceilinged and spacious, their big windows arranged in groups of threes. And the lavatories were huge. The floors in them were of black and white terrazzo and the windows reached up high, although the glass in them was the sort you can't see through but that lets light in. The Brobdingnagian urinals, made of ancient ceramic with thousands of hairline cracks, were taller than grown men. Standing at one of them, I felt as though I were staring at approximately the height of an imaginary belt buckle.

They called the first class of the day "home room," a term new to me. My own first class was Social Studies, and the teacher was named Miss Shuh. She was young and pretty and had light brown hair. The very first thing she did was tell all of us that her name was pronounced in exactly the same way as the word "shoe" and that if she ever heard anyone making fun of it there would be serious trouble.

One day much later in the year, Miss Shuh, as part of a project of one kind or another, handed out pieces of construction paper to her students and explained that each of us was to fold our sheet into thirds. I had become friends that year with Tommy West and Denny Gardner, both of whom swore incessantly and used obscenities frivolously, highly contagious habits to a boy like me of twelve years or so. As a consequence, in preparing my piece of construction paper for folding, I found myself half singing, lightheartedly and not *quite* under my breath, "Fold your sheets into turds." I liked Miss Shuh very much and recognize now that I had a bit of a boyish crush on her. I would never intentionally have done anything to displease her, let alone offend or enrage her. Not *intentionally*.

But this wasn't intent. This was habit, imitation, thoughtlessness. And from the front of the room Miss Shuh looked straight at me as if pinning me with a laser-beam, chin raised, blue eyes furious at the cowering, thoughtless little weasel who was the one, she knew perfectly well, who had spoken.

As I, too, knew perfectly well.

Strange, isn't it, that this memory should have stayed with me for as long as it has. I entered seventh grade in September of 1953. Seventy years ago. I remember the wonderful scent of the air that fall—the autumn I changed schools—the smell of drying leaves, the warmth of the sun. The year now is 2022. Miss Shuh couldn't possibly have passed fewer than twenty-one birthdays in order to be considered for the post of a seventh grade home room teacher. Perhaps more. That would make her now ninety years old at the least, assuming she's still alive. How unlikely that is, although certainly possible. Poor Miss Shuh. Dear Miss Shuh. How different things are now. The hallways of the West Tree Junior-Senior High School are gone altogether. The tall classroom windows are no more. And we, those of us still living, are surrounded by death in everything we see, and in everything we hear, just as we are, also, in everything that we remember.

4

1

Being Blind

He couldn't possibly have survived if he hadn't deceived himself that he was blind. Dirt and ugliness were everywhere he looked. Including the sight of his "leaders." Their airs, cruelty, smugness. How he despised them, their arrogant officialdom and pompous certainty. Criminals, all—except for some of the nurses, like the one who screamed at the unit supervisor and got "relieved" on the spot as a result. Erin. After the shaming and the termination, he found her crumpled in a corner of the wardroom, crying. Dark hair, young, very pretty. She held her hands up against her face. *Something very, very bad is going on*, she whispered to him, as if he alone were the one she must tell.

His own job was loading the refrigerated trucks that stood day and night, lining the streets outside. He never saw Erin again. But he thought of her every day for a very, very long time.

2

9/11

Lies are truth. Sickness is health. Fraud is candor.

Madness is sanity.

Such words and phrases were going through his head as he took the elevator down, passed through the foyer, then went out the front entrance of the building onto the sidewalk.

The morning was beautiful. The sky was clear and actually blue for once, not covered by the usual steel-gray haze that made it look as if skim milk had been poured into it. The air was fresh and pleasantly cool against his skin.

He walked down to the corner, where greetings came from the Yemini guys sitting outside their housewares store. The same came from Manuel at the flower stand. Manuel's cat, when he bent down to scratch her ears, rolled onto her back to welcome a belly rub.

He walked to the end of the block and got a large coffee from Lenny's Bagel Shop. Then he returned the way he had come, carrying the coffee past the cat, past Manuel, and past the Yeminis at their store.

When he was in his apartment again, in the front room, at his desk, coffee near at hand, he opened his computer, drew its keypad toward him, and typed two sentences:

"Today is May 20th, 2021. Our 'leaders' want all of us dead as soon as possible."

Sunday, September 11, twenty-one years after the crime. Television programs have been moved around, regular shows having been canceled to make time for the reading of the names of the three thousand who were "lost" twenty-one years ago today. Up is down, lies are truth, ignorance is wisdom. Those whose names are slowly read aloud, in alphabetical order, are designated "heroic sacrifices" by those reading their names and by the several million across the nation who know no better and have been told no other. For most of the population, habit and conditioning are a source of greater comfort than truth. The age of television. I think of their comfort as the sort enjoyed by a person demonstrably proud of being fit, hale, and able, unaware that death will come in a week, at most two, of a brain embolism.

.

The day is lovely, although the sky isn't the cloudless blue of twenty years ago, a hue it will never achieve again. This morning it's low and soft, a uniform gray. It seems to me subtly brooding, urging thoughtfulness, although at the same time I can't help but think of it as benevolent, as having a kindness about it. It hangs low, almost as if you could reach up and grab a handful of it. There is no wind. The temperature is warm. The sky-air is pleasant as it enters your lungs.

I'm surprised to find that the extra lane on Broadway—the "third lane" they created some years ago on the southbound side—is filled with empty parked cars. We have always been told that this lane is reserved for "emergency vehicles," fire trucks, for example, and the extraordinarily heavy traffic in ambulances. This particular day, however—as if no one falls sick on this day—will go by entirely without sirens. The parked cars belong to some of the thousands of off-duty officers who have come from the suburbs into the city to take part in the day's ceremonies.

·

I spend the morning at my desk and stay there until an hour past noon. The windows are open. Soft air comes in from time to time. The day is quiet, the city hushed. It is worshipping its swollen idol.

Around one-thirty I go downstairs and out the front door of my building. As I step onto the sidewalk, four officers in dress uniform brush by rapidly just in front of me. Even though I almost bump into them, or they into me, they don't notice me or look at me or pause or change their path. They continue striding briskly in the direction of West End Avenue and the Firemen's Memorial in Riverside Park.

As if through a silent and invisible spell, these officers have become anathema to me over the past two decades, as I have become anathema to them.

They, like millions of others, bought the lie and value it now as a man fallen overboard might value his lifejacket.

Therefore they are anathema to me.

I didn't buy the lie, and I don't buy it, and I don't value it.

Therefore I am anathema to them.

I have become their enemy.

No matter what I might say to them beyond simple amenities would be anathema to them. If we were to talk about the lie, they would prefer to abjure and crush me.

·

We are not free but everywhere in chains. I spent part of this warm, gray, early autumn day reading a book by Dr. Vernon

Coleman called *Social Credit: Nightmare on Your Street*. Coleman's little book is about the deceptions and falsehoods being used to enslave and then destroy us. "Everywhere in the world," writes the author, "the conspirators are fighting to gain power over us all." (p. 21)

A page or two later, Coleman adds, "By now you probably think I'm making this up and I wish I were but I'm not. We're not talking about the far distant future. We're talking about things that are happening now, or about to happen in the very new [*sic*] future." (p. 23)[1]

•

As I mentioned earlier, once a week, on Mondays at five, I meet with a small group of friends for what we call our "Literary Club." There, among other things, we exchange pieces of our own writing in order to analyze and evaluate them. Most of the time these are stories. In the past—during my "working years"—if someone happened to ask me what stories are, or what stories are supposed to do, I answered by saying that what they should do is tell the truth in a way that itself is also true. After that I would often be asked, "The truth about what?" I would answer that a story should tell the truth about existence. More exactly, it should tell the truth about the experience of being alive *inside* that existence.

That was a careful way of saying that stories should reflect the private, intimate experience of being conscious, thinking, feeling, and aware; and that they should do this in a way that itself is also true, real, complete, and accurate.

•

––––––––––––––––––

1 Dr. Vernon Coleman, *Social Credit: Nightmare on Your Street: What social credit means to you and how it will change your life*, 2022. Copyright Vernon Coleman June 2022. "The right of Vernon Coleman to be identified as the author of this work has been asserted in accordance with the Copyrights, Designs and Patents Act 1988."

One truth now about our existence is that we're at war. Most people, like the policemen, don't realize this. Coleman puts it this way: "This is a war between the informed and the ignorant, the courageous and the cowardly, the dignified and the undignified, the respectful and disrespectful. Unless we win this war we are all going to die except for the evil elite."

•

This struggle could not be more intense or more important: It is a struggle for the freedom, history, and dignity of human beings on the one hand; and it is a struggle for the destruction, subjugation, and lobotomized serfdom of human beings on the other.

•

Few know about this war. In one way or another, most choose not to know. Further, those who don't know, in general, despise those who do.

•

Hearing names read aloud at "ground zero" again this year; finding officers' cars parked where parking is "illegal"; seeing the quartet of uniformed men sweeping up my street—these were three small cracks in the "official" truth that has been woven around us through criminality and deceit.

We are at war.

Yesterday I saw and heard three hints of this war; three small things that albeit tiny revealed the presence of deceit, falsehood, power, and danger.

So that's the story, the story of seeing and hearing those things, that I will bring to the literary club tonight.

3

Small Potatoes

I've learned a good number of new names in the two-and-a-half—now three—years since the craven and sinister war against the world's people began. I used the words "craven" and "sinister." Permit me to add "cowardly" to that pair, making it a trio.

The aim of this sinister, craven, cowardly war is to kill off as many as possible of Earth's population, up to a limit that's satisfactory to the murderous, and surviving, elites.

How is this to be done? With a poison (called a "vaccine") that causes people's bodies to turn against them, resulting in death.

This result—death—can come about slowly or it can come about quickly. Many of the injected die abruptly. As for the rest, as Dr. Vernon Coleman wrote in 2021, "Most of the vaxxed will... be lucky to last five years."

A friend sent me an article reporting on a study done by the American Heart Association. It ran under this headline:

American Heart Association Report: Vax Spike Proteins Will Kill 50% of Youth, All Others With 1 Shot & Booster Most Will be Dead

by 2027 https://www.rumormillnews.com/cgi-bin/forum.cgi?noframes
%3Bread=215603

Most people deny that such a thing is happening. I am not one of them. I am more interested in why this enormous atrocity is happening than I am in pretending it doesn't exist.

I've already lost one friend, not because he died, but because he insisted on remaining in denial. For me, spending time with him became unbearable.

Trying to remain friends with him was something like this:

Imagine my friend and me on a passenger train. Imagine us sitting in the dome car having a glass of wine and, as always, discussing something philosophic or literary—Nietzsche, say, or Thomas Mann. The train is racing at a hundred-fifty miles per hour on shiny tracks. As it happens, my friend's seat faces the rear of the train. He can see the receding tracks, the scenery and the landscape disappearing backwards. My own seat faces in the opposite direction, toward the front of the train. I too can see the shining tracks, in this case as they reach out ahead. But I can also see that, not so very far out, these tracks cease to exist. They come abruptly to an end at the lip of a mile-high cliff. The cliff offers nothing but a straight drop to the jagged, rocky coastline and tossing sea below that will soon provide a resting place for the speeding train and every last one of its passengers.

Under such circumstances, my interest in Nietzsche or Thomas Mann decreases in inverse proportion to my intensifying interest in bringing the train to a stop at once.

Some of the names I have learned since the onset of the war are:

Michel Chossudovsky
Joseph Mercola
Mike Whitney

Dr. Vernon Coleman
Peter Koenig
Judy Wood
Emanuel Pastreich
F. William Engdahl
Eric Zuesse
Edward Curtin
Jon Rappoport
Judy Mikovits
Paul Edwards
Eric Walberg
Kees Van Der Pijl
Zina Cohen
Francis A. Boyle
Rhoda Wilson
Celia Farber
Naomi Wolf
Reiner Füllmich
Polly Tommey
Etc.

These are some of the people devoted to exposing the deceit and lies and to telling the truth about the programs of murder.

On the other hand, if a person were to list the names of those who support the lies and who therefore strengthen, reinforce, and make more efficient the program of mass murder—such a list of names would go on for pages and pages and pages, fill entire libraries, contain the ranks of ancient, revered, established professions, exhaust the rosters of schools, colleges, universities, and learned institutions across the land, as well as entire governments local, state, federal, and world, along with all of their departments and agencies, their research centers, training programs, presses, publishing houses, and on and on.

Compared with so huge a list as that, the earlier list is small potatoes.

In such a time as this, I can't help but feel that each day is ever so slightly more difficult than the one before. Knowing and reading about the truth, being a student of it—this kind of work is lonely, bringing few friends and little company. In fact, much of the time it diminishes your company, especially if you fail to keep a secret of the things you know. Suppose you're sitting next to someone at a bar, chatting amicably, and you say to this person that he or she is going to die within five years, perhaps sooner, and there's no escaping it. In my own experience, that person is likely to become angry or offended and consider you mad, is almost certain to move away from you, not want your company any longer, look at you suspiciously, and say denigrating things about you to others.

There is a person named Alicia Simmonds who has become this way toward me.

It is extremely frustrating and maddening, such a situation as this, when the population is being programmatically destroyed, yet at the same time it feels as if mentioning the truth about this fact has been made illegal. Each day seems in one way or another more restrictive than the day before. I continue to sit in my living room, near the window, where I work on these pieces of writing. I force myself to go out at least once each day, although almost never for as long as the day before. I walk less. Lately, in fact, I've gotten down to only a few blocks—to Broadway, down to 97th St., over to West End Avenue, then the two blocks back uptown. I tell myself I'm looking for the woman in the red coat, the woman with two children. But in truth I doubt she's alive anymore.

4

At War

I became acquainted with the brilliant although incorrigible Lance Crane when I overheard him, one night at dinner, mention the name "Judy Mikovits." This was at Regional restaurant last year, 2022, in the late fall. The weather was still warm enough to sit out on the front porch, or in what we more familiarly called "the shed," a roofed and open-aired but unpainted thing knocked together back in the time when it was still forbidden for people to gather indoors. There was room in the shed for half a dozen tables or so, and business that night was good enough that the tables were all taken. As a result, the place held a considerable amount of noise—voices, dishes, laughter. Lance Crane was in a group of four across from Barbara and me. The conversation from that group was animated and, at least by the sound of it, now and then argumentative. Lance Crane's voice isn't especially loud, nor is it deep, but Lance *does*—as I later found out all too well—have a tendency to pontificate, or, to put it another way, to keep on talking until another person gives up and stops. This seems to have happened in the shed that night. Three or four voices were all talking at once, and then, as abruptly as if the others had fallen off a cliff, there remained just one. And that one was Lance saying,

"If you want to find out, read Judy Mikovits."

As it happened, I myself had read Judy Mikovits and considered her one of the half dozen honest virologists left in a betrayed, ruined, and war-torn branch of science—and so when Barbara and I had finished dinner and were leaving the shed, I stopped at Lance's table.

"Apologies for intruding," I said. Then I added, "But I couldn't help but hear you mentioning one of my great heroes."

Just those few words and I was in the grip of Lance Crane forever. For years, I'd seen him in the neighborhood at one place or another, walking the bulldog that he addressed—so I was to learn—as his "Gatsby." He was tall, a head taller than me, and he seemed to have considerably more bulk above the waist than below. This impression of top-heaviness was greater in summer than in winter, when the imbalance would be disguised by the flowing, pleated, and belted trench coat he wore against the cold. Summer, though, was another matter. Warm weather brought him out in broken, worn, and dusty leather sandals, loose pleated shorts that hung not quite to the knee, and very thin short-sleeved cotton shirts with buttons straining visibly to stay closed against the pressure of a barrel chest and very generous belly. The shorts, though, were the greatest contributors to the appearance of top-heaviness, since the hairy but also rather thin lower legs exposed by the shorts gave the impression of being dangerously insufficient for supporting—let alone *balancing*—the enormous superstructure towering above them.

In my years of seeing Lance on the street, I had always harbored the suspicion—or the private hope—that he might in fact be the great liberal historian Webster Griffin Tarpley, whose books (those that I'd read) raised Tarpley to the same level of greatness in my own private pantheon as the one occupied by Judy Mikovits.

I mean no disrespect, but it was the size of the head that first made me think of Webster Tarpley. Lance's head, like Tarpley's, was large. But more notable in Lance's case was the almost perfect roundness of this part of his body. It was an almost exact replica of a basketball, albeit one with facial features visible on one of its curved surfaces and, of course, with ears on two sides.

In the weeks and months after my first words to Lance—and before I perfected a certain number of escape-and-evasion tactics—I became aware not only of the all-inclusive breadth of his extraordinary ideas but of the extreme urgency he apparently felt to convey these to others. It's true, as I said, that I'd noticed him for years on the street, but not until I spoke to him in the shed at Regional had he had the least reason to notice *me* in turn. Now, however, after I'd revealed to him my veneration of Judy Mikovits, he took to noticing me, as it were, in spades.

It used to be that if I happened to be waiting for the light to change so I could cross Broadway, *and* if I happened to see Lance and his dogs doing the same thing on the other side of the avenue—it *used* to be that I needed take no defensive maneuvers at all but that I could pass by Lance—and his dogs—smack in the middle of Broadway enjoying the armorlike protection of complete anonymity. We would pass by one another as though both of us were wholly invisible.

Now, though, from all the way across Broadway, he would make it clear by some gesture of the hand that he'd already seen me. With the change of the light, he would set out from his side and I from mine, with the result that we would pass one another, inevitably, on the island in the middle. And there, like a weaker magnet gripped by a stronger, I would find myself stuck for fifteen or even twenty minutes in a kind of force-field, listening to the horrors and revelations, to the gruesome, dreadful, apocalyptic certainties about government, nation, and world as they spilled forth from inside the large and very strange head of Lance Crane.

Now, as for myself, let me say at least this much: That I am indeed far from averse to participating in the tendencies or modes of perfectly logical thought that since the years immediately following the assassination of President Kennedy have been disparaged, belittled, demeaned, and misrepresented by our "leadership" as "conspiracy theory." I know that defaming reasonable and informed adult thinking as "conspiracy theory" is itself a crime against society, individual freedom, and both intellectual and personal liberty. To quote e. e. cummings' great poem "i sing of Olaf glad and big," "there is some shit I will not eat." I know perfectly well who killed President Kennedy and why they did so; I know perfectly well who killed Bobby Kennedy and why they did so; I know perfectly well who killed Martin Luther King and why they did so; I know perfectly well who destroyed the seven World Trade Center buildings and why (and how) they did so; and I know perfectly well who is perpetrating today's great Covid-19 terrorism and genocide campaign and why they are doing so.

I know these things and more.

But the things I know are as nothing compared to the things inside the capacious mind of Lance Crane. I know that President Biden is a weakling and a puppet; I know that he is a danger to liberty, that he is a liar, deceiver, and miscreant; I know that he is a danger to liberty, to life, to the people, to health, and to the world.

But to the alarmed and curious Crane, Biden is not even alive, but has been murdered by the true (and carefully invisible) leaders of our "government," and has been replaced by an actor who looks *just like* Biden and can be trusted implicitly (on pain of death) to do precisely and exactly as he is told by the true but invisible leaders of our "government."

This fate has been visited also upon Hillary Clinton and Kamala Harris, upon all of the cabinet members of the now also out-of-office President Donald Trump and numerous others, particularly those having held powerful or influential positions in the judicial branch, including Chief Justice John Roberts and Justice Clarence Thomas.

These are samples of the things I used to hear after being stopped through a tap on my shoulder by the urgent, needy, insistent Lance Crane, graduate of Yale University, holder of advanced degrees from Columbia University, inexhaustible researcher, reader, thinker, investigator—and seemingly crazed alarmist.

According to Lance, the true centers of government are the intelligence agencies themselves, which are actively planning for the shutdown of the entire world much along the lines of the lockdowns of nations, societies, and economies devastatingly imposed in the early months of the year 2020.

What is coming, however, will be much worse, more totalitarian, than anything we have seen so far.

Lance would come up to me in the half-secretive manner of a character in a grade-B spy movie and whisper to me,

"It may be sometime near the end of next week."

Something is wrong with Lance's left eye, causing the flesh surrounding it to squint, while the eye itself tends to roll outward, ignoring its companion on the right side of the round face.

As I said, I have developed ways of avoiding Lance, sometimes going so far as to cross the street, or even detour around a block, if I happen to see him approaching.

Tactics and evasions of such a kind have made life a little bit easier for me, or at least life as it has to do with Lance Crane. The real trouble, though, won't go away. Yes, Lance is a pest. He talks but doesn't listen, he doesn't converse but he preaches, if you take a step backward, to ease away from him, he takes a step forward. These things are true. But they're not the real problem, at least not for me. The real problem is that I agree with Lance Crane. Well, not about Biden and Harris and Clinton having been murdered and replaced by actors, but about the general horror and ruin of things, the lies and deceptions, the massive wrongs, the manipulations, the uses of terror, the lobotomizing of the people to make them compliant until such time, perhaps very soon, when they can be controlled totally. Yes, we are in a war. And it's a war against us, against we, against the people. But I don't want Lance Crane, or I don't want the likes of Lance Crane, to fight this war for me. No, to fight a serious defensive war, or to fight a serious defensive war with any hope of success at all, it's necessary to be completely and unremittingly sane.

5

War Story

For most of my life, grappling with the difference between thinking and telling has been a plague. From the day in eleventh grade when I first knew—realizing it with a clear certainty—that I wanted to be a writer, the difference between putting down thoughts or feelings on the page and putting down events never became quite clear to me. It certainly was never something I understood naturally. The truth is, in fact, that it was a much more difficult, and a much more unpleasant, task for me to tell "stories" than it was to explain, explore, or elucidate thoughts, feelings, moods, concepts, or ideas. One time after I had been writing for a couple of years—I was by then a freshman in college—I showed one of my pieces to a distinguished and august mentor who was in truth quite frightening to me. Still, frightened or not, I showed him what I was then calling a story. He returned it to me with little delay, handing it back with the comment that "nothing happened" in it and that it wasn't a story at all.

Something had to *happen*? But this was a story about jazz music, how much I loved it, what it felt like when I listened to it, how much I wished I could be a jazz musician myself (as well as a writer). But, still, something had to *happen*? This was a crushing blow. After all, the truth was that nothing *had* happened. And the truth also was that nothing ever *did* happen, not in *my* life. No, I loved the feel, the sound, the look, the very *scent* of New Orleans jazz, and I wanted nothing more than to be one of those who could play it and who lived with it *all the time.*

But my mentor said something had to happen. My mentor said that what I'd written wasn't a story. To me, the meaning was this: I couldn't write about my love of jazz music *and* write a story.

·

After a few years of struggling with this problem, I came to the conclusion that in actuality there *weren't* any stories, at least none that came my way, none that I could see or feel, none that made themselves palpable against *my* senses. There were only the extraordinarily abundant moods, settings, atmospheres, feelings that, as ever, I tried incessantly to put into words.

In time, I concluded that people who did write stories were able to do so only because they made them up. They fabricated the stories they told. For my own part, though, I wasn't interested in things that were made up. I wanted things that were real, and only those. I wanted things that were rich and supple and whole and intact, things that came from life directly, like music, things that were capable not only of impinging themselves on my senses and feelings, but of entering into my mind and into my body itself, the way music did, the way music couldn't help but do.

More years passed in this way, then decades. I wrote piece after piece and sent them off to magazines from which they would come back with the same unvarying comment, this being that the pieces I had submitted weren't stories at all but that they were "mood pieces," "fantasies," "prose poems," "studies." They weren't stories. However elegant the writing in them may have been, they were invariably in want of "narrative drive," or, as I remember once being told, they were lacking in "sinew."

•

As the years passed, it seemed increasingly clear to me that stories happened elsewhere, not to me. And the additional truth of the matter also become more and more clear: Stories didn't happen to *other* people, either, no more than they did to me. All of those other people's stories, the ones that were fabricated and made up—they weren't *real*, so how could they actually have happened to the people who "wrote" them and who implied that they had happened to them?

I came to an important, even extraordinary, recognition. Stories didn't happen to me any more than they happened to those other people, the ones who claimed they did but who in actuality made them up.

No, stories didn't happen to us. Instead, they happened to the *world*.

And most of them were awful. The world was having all kinds of stories happen to it, and most were terrible, having to do with injury and murder, destruction, killing, and ruin.

Many were stories of crimes against nature, otherwise known as the world's clothing, which in various cases was being burned, rent, poisoned, defoliated, desecrated, raped, rendered impotent, arid, and useless, then abandoned. Others were stories of the world's people, almost always stories about things done *to* those people rather than stories about things done *by* them. Sometimes these stories became widely known through a kind of instantaneous "publication," whereby a single conceit, image, sound, metaphor, or photograph of the story's presumed (often incorrectly) climax would serve as a means for audiences to "read" the story instantaneously. Examples might be the photo of a howling co-ed as she kneels over the dead body of a fellow college student just then killed by rifle fire; or the photo of a man in Saigon, his face contorted as he receives a bullet from the pistol someone is holding to his left temple and has just fired.

·

The strange and terrible thing about these stories, the ones being received by the world, has nothing to do with their being real or not. They are or were indeed, and they remain, real without any question. *These* stories aren't made up, manufactured, or spun out of thin air. No, these, unlike the others we've talked about, are real indeed. The terrible thing about them is that the people who "read" the world's stories—including me—aren't capable of *believing* their realness, let alone internalizing it. The reason for this deficiency is that a "reader" like me thinks of the world as something so large as to be outside of myself, so large as not to be of concern to me. These stories are *still* not stories that *I myself* am having. They're still not stories about *me*. No matter how visibly horrible her story may be, *I* am still not the howling co-ed, and what is happening to her isn't happening to *me*; and *I* am still not the man in the square in Saigon, and someone is not firing a bullet point-blank into *my* temple.

·

But things can change. And now, in fact, they *have* changed. Murderers have emerged in numbers never before seen or known. These are secretive murderers, evil and perverted, yet unremittingly determined in their aim to kill you and me. For the first time in my life I feel as though I do have a story, and that it's real, and that it actually is happening to *me*.

Everyone must have this same feeling.

If they know what's being done to them, that is, everyone must have this same feeling.

The trouble is, most don't know.

The fact is, though, that we're at war. The silent, lascivious, traitorous guns are pointed directly at us, making each and every one of us a doomed and meaningless hero.

What a story. I can only wish—only hope and pray—that in it nothing will happen.

6

October 2022

October 6, 2022. A calm, warm, sun-filled day. Two o'clock in the afternoon. I am again at my desk, at the open window, looking out over 99th Street—and thinking about death. I have known now for a considerable time that an immense insanity is sweeping across the earth. I have also known for a considerable time that this insanity exists in the form of a plot calculated to bring about the death of human populations with particular ruthlessness and on an unprecedented scale.

I have no idea what to do in the face of so monstrous a thing. I have tried writing—notes, letters, essays, a *book*—but I can find nowhere to publicize, let alone publish, such things. The mass media and all the attendant thought police—that is, all of the essential directors of and in the plot, including literary publishers—keep discussion and discourse, whether written or spoken, to a minimum while themselves generating as widely as possible their own lies and distortions in support of—or in malign neglect of—the secret and unprecedentedly destructive plot against the people.

One of the most unsettling things about the crisis is not

only the fact that almost no one has the least idea of what is being done to them, but they reject—at times scornfully, at other times witheringly, at still others angrily—efforts to introduce them to the truth of the situation, or attempts to talk with them about it.

These kinds of effort can be made with delicacy, subtlety, and politeness, and still be met with dismissiveness, scorn, or a righteousness often accompanied with anger, calumniation, or the making of actual threats against the person attempting to engage the other.

Observing this willful—even prideful—ignorance is something that fills me with fear. Never have I been as terrified as I am now of my own countrymen, fellow citizens, my own people. Imagine the existence of a certain kind of mask designed so as to be worn over the eyes, closing out every detail of what might be called "external reality" and leaving the wearer in total darkness. Then, however, imagine that this mask is able to do something further; imagine that it has the ability to provide, make visible, or project moving images—"movies," as we say—for the enjoyment of the mask's wearer—and imagine further that these movies are excellent in execution and in quality, that they are captivating, compelling, engrossing, comforting and invariably rewarding to the ignorant wearer of the mask. Imagine that this mask remains over the wearer's eyes not just some of the time but all of the time, day and night, morning and noon, during sleep and during waking time, providing a perfect and unbroken continuity of pleasure, certainty, confidence, and delight to its wearer.

And *then* imagine what might, or would, happen if someone other than the wearer—if *you*, for instance, or if *I*—were to approach the wearer and, however gently or politely or delicately, begin to pry the mask away from that person's eyes....

•

It is now almost six o'clock and I am still here, at my desk, near the window, gazing down over 99ᵗʰ Street. I find myself imagining that the young woman in the red dress is about to pass by as she did before. No. What I just said isn't quite honest. In truth I find myself imagining not that she is about to pass by *again* but that she is about to pass by for the first time, with her two children, and that I will look at them and find myself wishing, hoping, desiring that they not disappear, ever.

7

My Country, 'tis of Thee

October 13, 2022. Again, near two in the afternoon. The air drifting in now and then through my window is balmy and aromatic. As it has been all day, the sky is covered by a light but unbroken overcast. Every ninety minutes or so a mist falls softly for a quarter of an hour, then disappears, leaving behind the smell called "petrichor," from the Greek words for "stone" and "ichor." This is a smell I associate with spring, as I suppose most people do. And so it disorients me, mixing up feelings of October with those of May.

I suppose this kind of confusion is appropriate to the way I'm feeling. The British might use the pronoun "one" at this point, mightn't they, as in "One feels at once a crippling anxiety at the prospect of an inhuman future and a paralyzing grief at the loss of the past."

Devastatingly well put.

Three-quarters of a century ago, Orwell wrote some words along the same lines, referring to the character of Winston Smith: "The past was dead, the future was unimaginable. What certainty had he that a single human creature now living was on his side?"

·

A memory has stayed with me from long ago. A Sunday morning in 1950, sometime around the first of the year. I am nine years old and lying on the living room carpet in the farmhouse my family then lived in, looking through the rotogravure section of the Minneapolis paper. The magazine's cover poses a question, and below it is an expansive but highly detailed illustration. The question is, "In Fifty *More* Years What Will The Future Hold?" And the illustration below it depicts an urban scene of extremely tall spire-like buildings piercing up into a cloud-swept sky that's crowded with hovercraft of various sizes, all of them shaped like pharmacists' capsules. Many of these are moored to the buildings at various heights in order to discharge and take on passengers, whom you can see as they pass through transparent tubes connecting the airships to the buildings. Very far below, the streets are also protected from the weather by some kind of transparent roofing, as are the sidewalks. Well-dressed people stand on the sidewalks but appear to be taking no steps, as if being carried along by the moving walkways themselves. On the streets are very few cars, while bus-like vehicles—also transparent—glide in and out of various lanes, picking up and discharging passengers.

·

More than seventy years have gone by since I studied that picture—and then afterward, however well I may have remembered its details, thought no more about it. In some fundamental way it wasn't true, anyhow. It had about it, instead of real thought, the cartoon whimsy of a theme park futurism.

Seventy years, though, is coming close to a hundred, and everyone thinks of centuries as significant markers of change. We're now a fifth of the way through the century we call the twenty-first, and it does seem unarguable that the future has been, is being, realized all around us. But this future isn't apparent through the way things look or the way people travel. It's apparent instead through manifestations of generalized ignorance, malevolence, and extraordinary evil.

The truth is that the future hasn't arrived at all. Instead, the past has been lost.

.

Just think. Consider the past carefully. It has been ignored, maligned, treated with insupportable indignities on such a scale, to such an extent, and for so long a time that it has at last died, disappeared, dried up, ceased to be. And the consequences of this disappearance are immeasurable to what was once called "humanity." This is because, without a past to give it birth and then to provide it with the nourishment and sustenance necessary for it to continue, the future can neither be born nor can it exist.

This is all our own fault. Thanks to our own massive failures in care, study, husbandry, and cultivation, thanks to our ignorance, shallowness, greed, laziness, and folly, what we have come to possess is a state of "past-lessness," an ongoing present with neither a generative past preceding it nor a future—with its potential for significance—coming after it. As a result, our species is alone, without support either from behind or from ahead. Each of us is bereft of the knowledge, resources, and direction that were once available from the past; and certainly we are bereft of such guides as might be available from the future, since that desired state will never, can't ever, now, come into existence.

•

You don't see them taking place, these myriad depravities. They occur out of sight, behind closed doors, in doctors' offices, in examination rooms, in hospitals, at other times inside the walk-in tents stretched over poles and set up at street corners or along curbsides, although these quickly become familiar and go unnoticed—except by those, the many, who still don't understand what is happening and regularly make use of these flimsy structures, entering to accept the services offered by the two or three white-coated workers inside. The fearsome depravities take place also in classrooms and lecture halls, in board rooms and recording studios, on movie lots and research laboratories, in fact in any place where ideas are exchanged—or lies are.

As a schoolboy I experienced dread for long periods of time, suffering through unshakeable fears as to what sort of terrors the future was going to hold. I convinced myself that I would recognize this future when it finally arrived, that I would sense a dreadful change like the ones hinted at in the various books that came my way, even in one or another single ominous sentence, a sentence, for example, like "It was a bright cold day in April, and the clocks were striking thirteen." But I was quite wrong about this. The terrifying thing now is that the future *won't* come, that it never will come, and that we must remain fixed in this cruelly poisoned emptiness of a murderous present, managing somehow to endure here until at last, one followed by another, in absolute silence, we will all have disappeared.

5

1

November 22, 1963

The afternoon following the president's murder was, for me, banal, flat, and empty. Coming out of Jessup Hall after fourth hour, I saw that people were holding transistor radios to their ears. I tapped someone's shoulder and asked what was going on. The person held his radio a few inches away from an ear and said, "The president has been shot," then put the radio back and went on, frowning with attentiveness. I had no radio of my own, neither in a jacket pocket nor back in my room. But I knew there was a television in the student union, so I walked there, down the bluff, and went inside. People were standing several deep in front of the television. I couldn't get close enough to make out what was on the screen or hear the sound, at least not clearly. An unusually tall fellow next to me was looking over the heads of the crowd and also holding a radio against one ear. I asked him what he was hearing. "It's not believable," he told me. "The president is dead."

Like everyone else, I had no idea what to do. I thought vaguely of going back to my room, but then I heard someone call my name. It was Fritz Dreisbach, talking to a black-haired, gaunt-looking person I didn't know. The gaunt person was wearing a very long raincoat, also black. I went over to them and Fritz said to me,

"I expect you already know."

"Almost nothing," I said. "They shot him. I heard he's dead. I can't believe it."

The other person gave Fritz a soft cuff on the upper arm, said "Later," gave me a sort of wave with two fingers, and turned away. For a second or two I watched him go. His black coat almost touched the floor, like a robe.

"Who was that?" I asked Fritz.

"Condorelli," he said. "You don't know Condorelli? Over in comp lit they call him The Raven, those tight-asses. I like him. A ghost from the Left Bank circa 1900. But listen," he changed the subject. "I'm picking up Peter Hatch and Bob Lehrer. We're going out to Jim Petzky's place. Couple six-packs of beer. Petzky's got writer's block. He's talking about suicide. Have you ever met his wife? A total sweetheart. Come along with."

My initial reaction was to turn him down. All of this took place now many decades ago, but I remember it perfectly. I knew that I didn't want to be off-campus, certainly not out of town.

By this time, news had gotten out that classes were canceled for the day, so I had no worries about missing my seminar in narrative theory. It was just that I didn't want to go all the way out to Petzky's. What I wanted was to learn more about the assassination. I wanted to go someplace where I could sit in a corner and listen to what was being said, perhaps a place with a television set. After that, I could move on to another corner, maybe at Kenney's, in the back, where I could watch them play pool and have a beer and listen to whoever was talking. But I knew I didn't want to leave town.

And I knew absolutely that I didn't want to get into a car. The atmosphere of doing either one of those things was entirely out of keeping with the complicated way I was feeling.

On the other hand, I had no other close friends, I mean other than Fritz himself and, to a much lesser extent the few I'd met through him—including Peter Hatch and Bob Lehrer. And of course Petzky, whom I liked very much. On balance, being with other people might offset the negative—the empty—aspects of leaving town.

So I accepted Fritz's invitation, though reluctantly, knowing that I was doing the wrong thing. I knew that for the remainder of the afternoon I would feel out of place, uncentered, above all unprotected, exposed.

Still in the student union, I leaned with my back against the long bank of phone booths and watched people pass by while Fritz called the others and arranged when and where to pick them up. Then I walked with him downriver to the long-term parking lot across from the hydraulic engineering building. His car was in the row farthest away, backed up against the scrub- and weed-grown railroad embankment there. We got in, drove out of the lot, headed uptown, and picked up Peter Hatch and Bob Lehrman as agreed, from the corner where they were standing in front of the Airliner.

Iowa City isn't a big town but it is a coherent one, or at least it was then. What I'm calling coherence was the quality about the town—and campus—that gave me the feeling of security and protection that I'd come to understand, even though this was my first autumn there, as something I craved deeply.

The town was somewhat curiously shaped. Instead of following the river, upstream and down, as you might have expected it to, it was formed more like an egg lying with its small end on the west side of the river and its large end swelling out on the east side.

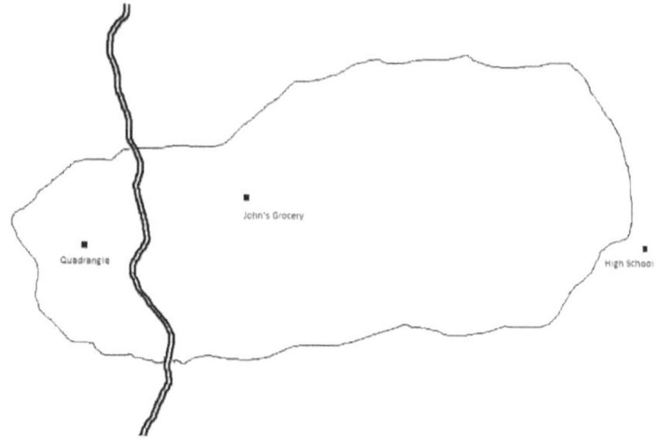

The shell of the egg was the city's periphery. Once you went outside of the periphery, protection ended.

Petzky lived in a subdivision a number of miles east of town, meaning that we would definitely be passing out through the eggshell. A few blocks after picking up Peter Hatch and Bob Lehrman, we stopped at John's Grocery, and I went inside with Fritz. The radio was on at a low volume with news and updates from Dallas. The counter clerk said that Lee Harvey Oswald had been arrested and that a Dallas cop had been shot dead. I know now that this was the beginning of the long and unbroken chain of lies that reaches all the way from then up to this present moment, as I write these words, late one April afternoon in 2028.

Fritz and I came out of John's Grocery with a wooden case of twenty-four beers for John's unmatchable price of $6.20 plus deposit. I held the case while Fritz unlocked the trunk, and then together we set it inside. While we were gone, Peter Hatch had gotten out of the back seat and was sitting now in the front passenger seat, where I had been sitting before. I ignored the move and got into the back. Without turning around, Peter said,

"I hope you don't mind, Mac. It's just I get car sick if I sit in back."

"No difference to me," I lied, or white-lied. Peter was a heavy person, maybe seventy-five pounds over what he should have been. It would have cost him an effort to turn around in the seat. He had double chins, a perfectly oval face, and a mouth whose default setting was the shape of a small letter "o."

Fritz set out on Market Street, took a left on Linn, another left onto East Jefferson, then a right onto Muscatine, after which we just kept on going. There wasn't much of any talking. Beside me in the back seat, Bob Lehrman sat looking out the side window, holding his transistor radio to his left ear. Fritz's car radio was broken.

I wasn't about to let any of them know what sort of discomfort I was going through. They wouldn't understand it, or, more likely, wouldn't believe it. Or would scorn it. They would say—Peter Hatch would say—that if I had fears about leaving town I shouldn't have come along.

I could identify almost exactly the moment we broke through the eggshell. Being aware of this point, where protection and safety ended, required keeping an eye on various other things—the number and density of trees (even when most of them were without foliage), the depth of the lawns leading back to the houses, and of course the size and design of those houses, their age and upkeep, how far apart they stood from one another (inside the eggshell it was as though they were less afraid of each other and made a less foolish pretense of seeming to stand alone), and, of course, the presence of sidewalks. When sidewalks ended, you were definitely outside the perimeter.

We broke through the eggshell as Fritz turned left from Muscatine Avenue onto East Court Street. This was a turn that took us past the wide, low, empty, treeless field of the new Iowa City high school, with its enormous parking lots and cutely meandering "roads." Clearly, we were no longer in town. We were on farmland. That is, farmland that had been adulterated, abused, and transformed. Taken from those who had tilled and dwelled on it previously, it had been stripped, scraped, bulldozed, and re-formed—exorcised of the last vestige of the life it had had before and made ready thus to receive the blandishments of the builders, planners, and financiers who now controlled its fate. What had been a "place" had been made into an "area," something with neither rigor, form, history, depth, mystery, nor dignity, something bland enough to be instantly "likable" to all and as a result wholly absent of overtones of seriousness or authority. No one was expected to find any objection to such an "area." No one was expected to do other than approve of it and, civic-mindedly, be grateful for it. On the other hand, it would never age well. It would never endure long enough to provide the solace of oldness or the unique pleasure that comes from the well worn. The building and this "area" would never age, but instead they would deteriorate. They wouldn't mature but they would fail to last. They wouldn't age gracefully or with increasing strength, but they would be touched, first in small ways and then in large, by decrepitude. They would become "outmoded" before they became old. The entire project would need "replacement." In these ways, the school represented the values and aims of its nation and era: It was not a project dedicated to dignity or permanence, but it was a project dedicated to plunder.

The men who built this school are the men who murdered John Kennedy.

I said nothing about any of this to the others in the car. None of them would agree with me in any case.

We drove another mile or two past more examples, not of schools, but of buildings, restaurants, banks, show rooms, car dealerships, home furnishing centers, all of them structures and places whose deterioration was built into their reason for being. My sense of vulnerability and exposure grew more pronounced the farther we went, an unease exacerbated by my inability to find any coherence in the scene. No single thing was related to any other. Flags, banners, and colored pennants flew over a lot filled with cars parked side by side, sale-prices on their windshields, while next to the car lot was a mortuary, next to the mortuary a restaurant called "Ribs 'n Chicks," next to the restaurant a windowless liquor store made of cement blocks, and so on.

It all meant that we were on destroyed farmland. Ever since breaking through the shell we had been on destroyed farmland.

And, of course, the farmland had stood on what was once native prairie.

Petzky and his wife lived in a very small one-story house in a string of half a dozen others like it in what had once been a tiny town but was now a large subdivision called Eden Lake. Their house lacked a curb, sidewalk, or garage, but it did have a driveway. Petzky's car was parked in it, and Fritz pulled up behind until the bumpers were touching. We got the beer from the trunk and all went inside.

Fritz was right about Petzky's wife being a sweetheart, though that word was too cheap to suit her. Her name, Rhoda, didn't fit her very well, either, a name too big, heavy, old, and round. She should have been named April, Rose, Fawn, or May, although none of those would really have been right, either. It's true that she was small, trim, not slight but almost so, and extraordinarily pretty. At the same time there was a seriousness about her that may actually have been her most pronounced trait. She was far too smart to be missing a sense of humor, but she was also far too smart not to know when to use it and when not to use it. I liked her very, very much.

As for Petzky, I already knew him well—in fact, I knew him better than I did any of the three I'd driven out with, excepting Fritz. Petzky wasn't on the scholarly side of degree-getting, so I didn't see him in Old English, but he was aiming for a degree in fiction-writing, so I did see him every Friday in the seminar on the theory of narrative we were both taking—and where we would be now if it weren't for the assassination.

Petzky was affable and smart, not to mention, with his

chiseled face and tight-curled black hair, tremendously good-looking. He came from Fayetteville, Arkansas, where he had gone to the university, and he was modest and quiet, never affected or ostentatious, and above all in possession of an excellent albeit quiet sense of humor. He'd come to Iowa City for the writing program, but now it appeared that he was badly stymied with his fiction and was becoming afraid he might be dropped.

When Rhoda opened the door to us, she said to him over her shoulder and across the tiny living room, "Jim, your rescue team is here."

I'll leave out the greetings and introductions, along with the regrets, comments, and expressions of disbelief about Dallas, though we did turn to Bob Lehrer for the latest update, since only when Rhoda opened the front door had he taken his transistor from his ear and put it in his pocket—and then only for a minute or two. There wasn't any television set in the living room, and, although I thought there might be one in the bedroom, I saw later that there wasn't one there either. After a time, this absence had a certain calming effect on my anxiety and my fear at having traveled outside of the eggshell: being in this tiny little house with five other people and no television. It may even have been that, for a time, I forgot where I was and what day it was. Before long, though, I had to go to the bathroom—the beer—and the earlier feelings came tumbling back. The bathroom was just big enough for a toilet, sink, and shower stall, although it did have a small square window. I stood for a moment looking out through it. Jim and Rhoda's house had no backyard at all, and a farmer's cornfield came up to within a foot or so of the house. By this time of year, the corn had been harvested, and as far as I could see there were only dry and broken stalks. A quarter-mile away or so stood an immense pylon with power lines hanging from its shoulders. Another quarter-mile away was another, and another beyond that. With their immense weight the power lines sagged down low between each tower.

The floorplan of Jim and Rhoda's house consisted of a plain rectangle, with a little more than half of its area devoted to the living room and the remainder split into the bedroom and kitchen, with space cut out of one corner of the kitchen to allow for the bathroom. Except for individual trips back and forth to get more beers, or to go to the bathroom, the group stayed in the living room for the afternoon. A couch stood against one wall, with room enough on it for three people, and, across from it, in a corner, sat an easy chair. Diagonally across the room from the front door were the straight chair, card table, and typewriter where Jim spent most of his time. And, once we all got settled, that's where he stayed, though he did turn the chair at a right angle to the table and lean it back on two legs so he was resting against the wall. I sat at one end of the couch, Fritz at the other, and Bob Lehrman in the middle. Peter Hatch had gone straight for the easy chair when we came in, and he continued to sit there, with his mouth in its shape of a small "o." Rhoda brought in a kitchen chair. I offered to trade it for my place on the couch but she said no, she was fine, and, besides, she had to go out before long.

Everyone had a beer, and we made a handful of rather muted toasts. Fritz proposed one to health and then another to hope. Bob Lehrman proposed that we drink to the assassinated president. Afterward there was some more talk about Dallas, although no one knew very much. By this time, on the jetliner, with Jackie standing beside him in the dress that had blood on it, Johnson had raised his big hand and taken the oath of office. None of us, at the time, knew that from that moment we were doomed. With a sigh, Fritz got up from his end of the couch and, gathering empties, took orders for another round. He came back from the kitchen with a bottle for everyone except Rhoda, who announced that if she didn't go shopping she wouldn't be able to feed Petzky that night. There was some laughter. I asked Rhoda where she went for shopping.

"The strip," she said casually.

"Oh, oh, I've got you parked in," Fritz said suddenly. "I'm right up to your bumper."

There was a change in the feeling of things as Fritz went out to move his car and Rhoda gathered up her belongings in preparation to leave. When she was ready to go, Petzky got up from his chair and went out the front door with her. I got up from the couch and went to follow, but the door fell shut on its own and I decided to step to the right, instead, and look out the picture window. Fritz's car was now parked on the street, and he, Petzky, and Rhoda were standing together at the open door of Petzky's car. At one point they all laughed. Then Rhoda got in and shut the door. She rolled down the window and she and Petzky exchanged a goodbye kiss. Then she started the car and backed down and into the street. The other two, hands in pockets, stood watching until she was out of sight. Then they turned to come back in. Meanwhile, no one in the living room had said a thing. Peter Hatch was still sitting in the easy chair, scowling around the room. Bob Lehrman, not having moved from the middle place on the couch, had his transistor against his left ear, listening intently.

With Rhoda gone, everything felt different, somehow looser and less constrained. Anyone who wanted a beer went into the kitchen and got it for himself, except for Peter Hatch, who invariably asked someone else to bring one for him. Conversation drifted away from the assassination and onto the subject of books and writing—specifically, the subject of Petzky's writer's block. For better or worse, the beer made the conversation flow more easily than it had seemed to before. Petzky was still sitting at the card table, but he sat now on four legs, no longer tipped back against the wall. I remember precisely the words he used, once the conversation was fairly well advanced.

"I swear to jesus. I sit here all day. I try and try and try and try. Damn. God damn. I sweat *bullets* trying to get a story going. Rhoda can tell you. I swear, I sweat *bullets*. I'm damn near ready to kill myself."

No one was quite certain what to say or do.

"Write a story about you and Rhoda," Fritz said after a moment. "An allegory. You can call her Sally Forth. And you can be called Holden Bach."

The beer was taking over. No one was really serious anymore. Even Peter Hatch stirred himself. Leaning forward in the easy chair, he said,

"No, no. Better yet, give Rhoda the name Manifest Destiny. That's as good as Holly Golightly, even better. Then all you have to do is follow her doings. Damn, that's a story that would write itself."

Conversation broke down. The beer had won. Fritz asked Bob Lehrman what news he was hearing on his transistor radio. I got up from the couch, went over to Petzky, and tried to tell him how awful I thought Peter Hatch's idea was. It was getting close to five o'clock by now. If it hadn't been for the assassination, Petzky and I would now have been ending up our theory of narrative seminar. We often went up to Kenney's for a beer after the class, and then Petzky would head back out to Eden Lake and I would walk across the river to the Quadrangle, where I would make it just in time for dinner.

Petzky stood up from his chair. I gave him a bear hug and said I'd be counting on seeing him next week, or, actually, the week after that, because of Thanksgiving.

It was time to go. I went out into the kitchen and came back with the case of empties, far lighter than before. Fritz had brought his car back up into the driveway, and I stood at the rear of it while he unlocked the trunk so I could set the empties in. Everyone shook hands with Petzky and offered good luck along with thanks and farewells. With nothing said, Peter Hatch got into the front passenger seat. Bob Lehrer and I got in back. Fritz got in last, after saying something more to Petzky. He backed down into the street and we set out. Petzky stood at the top of the driveway watching us go, the same as he and Fritz had stood watching when Rhoda drove off.

No one said anything for a minute, and then Bob Lehrman surprised me by saying, "Jesus Christ, I wouldn't live out here to save my fucking soul."

Fritz gave a big sigh. "I know what you mean," he said. "But I also know it's cheap. Petzky gets that whole little house on the prairie for forty-five bucks a month. Rhoda included."

We had come to a red light that kept us from turning onto the strip. Cars flashed by in front of us, going to the left and right. The light seemed to last forever.

I surprised myself by saying something that I instantly regretted. "I don't see how he could ever expect to write, out here in deadland."

Peter Hatch gave a contemptuous snort. "A person can write anywhere," he said. Then he added, "If they're a writer."

The light changed, thank god, and I was able to ignore the condescension in what Peter Hatch had said, or at least able to pretend I hadn't heard it. But I had heard it. As for me, I had been extraordinarily stupid. Thinking of my friend Petzky, I had said something I actually meant, something I actually thought to be true. But not so to Peter Hatch. It was as if I had slapped down five pounds of bloody red meat in front of a lion. Gone in an instant. It must have been delicious to him, his implicit insult and condemnation of Petzky. Now his smugness and gloating.

I swore to myself that I wouldn't say a word more during the remainder of the trip, not so much as a morpheme, not a phoneme. If need be, I would press myself into the corner of the back seat and pretend to be asleep. After all, imagine what would happen if I actually said more about the truth of my feelings. Not just about Petzky, but what if I actually explained my dread about leaving town, the feelings of uncertainty, vulnerability, and exposure, if I actually told them about the eggshell, or actually said that the high school was intended to deteriorate and had been built in dishonesty, only for plunder, or that nothing was logically related to anything else along the strip, that nothing connected to anything else, that the result was desperation, emptiness, and purposelessness, that the men who had built all these things had built them not for any good but solely for their own gain, investments in plunder, just like the men who offered Johnson the oath of office in exchange for his part in the killing of the president, dooming all of us to the death-in-life that our nation has now inevitably become.

I've drifted far away, I know, from that late afternoon in November of 1963 and the back seat of Fritz's car. At that time, a week away from turning twenty-two, I could never have used words the way I did just now. I couldn't possibly have known what the outcome of the assassination would be. But six decades have passed. And I've spent that time, for the most part, reading and watching. What has happened is beyond terror.

I have never abandoned my concept of the eggshell, although this is the first time I've ever revealed it.

I could feel it when we came back through the eggshell and were on the inside of it again. A sense of relief. Fritz swung by John's grocery, and, as I had volunteered to do, I got the case of empties from the trunk and took it inside for the dollar-twenty refund. Back in the car we split the money four ways. We all lived in the Quadrangle, but neither Bob Lehrman nor Peter Hatch wanted to go to the trouble of taking the car all the way back to the long-term lot, so Fritz let them off at the foot of the bridge. I moved into the front seat and we rode to the lot. Fritz parked again as far in the rear as he could. There was a free spot against the railroad embankment, like before, and he backed into it slowly until the bumper touched dirt and shrubs. We got back to the Quadrangle with ten minutes to spare before they closed the dinner line. There was no sign of Bob Lehrman or Peter Hatch.

Fritz lived in a room on first-floor south as opposed to mine on second floor north, so after dinner we checked our mail and then split up. I walked across the inner courtyard over to the north entrance. Almost every room I could see had lights on inside the windows. Maybe two or three were dark. In my own room I turned on only the goose-necked desk lamp, bent it down low, and sat down in the wooden chair. Like Petzky, I turned the chair so it was at a right angle with the desk and I could rest one arm on the desktop. I raised my feet up and used the left arm of the upholstered chair for a place to rest them. I was looking toward the two windows. One was cranked open an inch or two; the other was closed. They showed only blackness outside.

The eggshell was a wonderful thing in that you were equally protected wherever you happened to be, so long as you were inside it. Here, now, in my room, at my desk, I was positioned quite far toward the small end, but I was just as secure here as I would be if I were on the other side of town, so long as I was inside the perimeter.

Everything about it had to do with coherence, with the way things were related one to another, and then one to another again, the way they were intended to be. I had my room, my classes, my books—most of the books were stacked on the two rear corners of my desk. I had classes, hours, schedules, assignments. All of this had to do with the reason there could be meaning and significance on the inside, while on the outside plunder, chaos, and emptiness. I wondered what the others would think of such an idea. Fritz might possibly understand it, but not the others, including poor old Petzky. Certainly not Peter Hatch. But that was all right. None of them was ever going to hear a word about it, at least not from me. It was a secret I would take to my grave.

2

Failure

I've never said this to anyone, but all my life I have been frightened by the prospect of travel. This fear, whether of a trip planned for great distances or small, manifested itself in one form of illness or another, never severe enough to be noticeable to others, but enough so as to be discomfiting—*and discomforting*—to me.

Given this predilection, it could be expected that I might find relief in the fact that my life has now become more localized than ever before. Not only do I seldom leave my neighborhood, but I have restricted myself bit by bit to a very small part even of that, most of the time to an area comprising perhaps three or four blocks, possibly five.

Naturally, I am happy to be free of my old fear of travel— but I regret that it has been replaced of late by a new and different kind of fear, more deadly than what came before it. This new manifestation is withering, ominous, and all but omnipresent. It comes not from the act of moving from one place to another, as my old fear did, but it comes *to* me, instead, and it comes from everywhere; from extremely loud noises as much as from midnight's dead silence; from *within* the very things, objects, and structures, even the *feelings*, that make up the very stuff of life every second of the day.

How ironic it is that now, when I'm able at last to enjoy freedom from my old fear by exposing myself only to small things and tiny distances—how ironic it is that, just *now*, the world itself has changed in such a way that fear, pain, death, and terror seep invisibly out of every curbstone and crack, every lamp post and fire hydrant, every alleyway and window, every brick, hallway, latch, and door, every screen, every face, every pair of eyes.

Yesterday afternoon I decided I would go out for two or three items—a block of cheddar, a few tomatoes on the vine, a link of soppressata—and even in that short trip I realized how little it was true that I could possibly live a life free of fear.

The day was cloudless, bright, and still, but nowhere nearly as warm as the days of the few previous weeks, with their luxuriantly sweet smells of early autumn, a scent now swept away by the colder air.

At Broadway I turned right, passed the hardware store and then continued past the outdoor flower stand, past the health food store, after that past the two abandoned stores with their front windows looking like blind sockets, the two leaning shoulder-to-shoulder as if neither had the strength to stand alone. I proceeded then to 98th Street and, on the corner there, Lenny's Bagels.

That's when I saw the beggar I call Bogart. He was thirty or so feet ahead of me, having already crossed 98th Street and limping his way, slowly and as if painfully, toward the entrance of the same supermarket where I myself was headed.

I knew that if I crossed 98th Street I would overtake him within just a few strides, and I didn't—I made this decision in a nano-second—want to meet him just now, since he would plead for more money than the dollar or two I was willing to hand him. So I pivoted on my right foot ninety degrees and set out on 98th Street toward West End Avenue.

I call him Bogart because of his handsome, drawn, sadly hangdog face, like Bogart's, although in no other way is he a likeness. I have no idea what may have happened to him in the past, but his teeth—at least the three that protrude and are visible—are stained a coffee brown, he's skinny as a junkyard rat, has no easy time forming words when he tries to talk, and his right leg has apparently no knee joint at all but hangs down straight from the hip and makes much more of an impediment than an aid to walking.

Still, along with all this, he has eyes of a piercing gemlike green. Mournful, expressive, deep, the most stunningly beautiful eyes.

·

Halfway through the block toward West End Avenue there was an obstruction in the street. I stepped out from the curb to see what it was. An "Access-a-Ride" van was trying to squeeze through between the parked cars on the north side of the street and a double-parked car on the south. I stepped out in front of the van to see how much clearance the driver had, but just as I'd gotten my sight-lines in place he managed to squeeze through. I stepped back to the curb, up onto the sidewalk, and stood there for a moment. I realized suddenly that I felt depressed, curiously frightened, and for some unknown reason ashamed. These feelings were all manifestations of "the fear."

·

The corner of West End and 98th gave me the sense that I was in a different neighborhood, even a different city, from my own. It was because of the sunlight, I think, and the way it reflected off the buildings. A memory of Paris flashed through my mind, then another, this one of Vienna. Two women stood nearby, back to back, four or five feet away from one another. Each held a cell phone to one ear. And each, in her free hand, held onto a leash. At the end of each leash a small dog tugged and pulled. While the women talked on their telephones, the dogs strained toward one another, barking, nipping, and growling.

.

I crossed 98th Street and turned left to return to Broadway. At almost mid-block, I heard someone call my name, pulling me from a revery about my ex-friend Jonathan Fried, whose front door I was within a few feet of passing. At the sound of my name, I turned to see someone approaching me from the north side of 98th Street. He was tall and wore a brimmed hat. A black surgical mask covered the bottom half of his face.

I was absolutely certain that I had never seen him before in my life.

As he came up to me, something hesitant about his manner gave me the distinct impression that he suddenly felt as though he had never seen me before in *his* life either.

But if that were true, how would he have known my name? Did I look exactly like someone else who happened to have my first name?

"Hello and how are you?" the man asked.

"Just getting a little exercise," I lied, "on my way to the store."

"Yes," he said. "And what a day. It's an absolutely perfect day for it, isn't it."

I couldn't see his eyes, since he was wearing dark glasses of a deep green. The opaque lenses were oversized, big as lemons, and perfectly round, giving him a startled, clownlike appearance.

It seemed to me that he tipped his head slightly to one side, inquisitively, before he turned away.

•

It becomes clear to me at this point that I have failed badly. With whatever hopes I may have set out at the beginning of this piece of writing, I realize now that I have failed in them, miserably. None of what I've written so far is true—or at least not altogether true. There really is a crippled-up derelict with green eyes whom I call Bogart because of his mournful looks. And I really did avoid him last Thursday by going out of my way, over to West End and back again. There really was an "Access-a-Ride" van squeezing through a tight spot on 98th, and there really were two women at West End with two cell phones, two leashes, and two nipping and over-excited dogs. I really did think of Paris, and then of Vienna, for a second or two, and someone really did call out my name and cross over the street. It's a lie, though, that I didn't know who that person was, even though the rest of what I wrote is more or less true (although he *wasn't* wearing a surgical mask; on the other hand, I never really did understand why he'd crossed the street to my side of it). I really did pass the front door of "my ex-friend Jonathan Fried," and I really did think I would write about the end of our friendship and explain why it is that he and I no longer see one another, a matter having to do with the fear I've been talking about—but I suddenly realized that what I had set out to write about, what I was really trying and hoping to write about, had gotten away from me completely. It was eluding me hopelessly. It was escaping like a jack rabbit running farther ahead of me the more I myself tried to run in order to catch it.

It would be better to quit; stop writing; admit failure; fall silent.

What I intended to write about at the beginning of this piece was the fear, the one different from my old fear of travel. Fear of travel is fear of the unknown, but this new fear comes from what one *knows*. And so murderous is what I know—

immense, ruthless, diabolical, unscrupulous, inhumane—that it has grown into the unspeakable. And so I must remain mute, imprisoned inside the iron-barred impossibility of so much as describing or identifying it, this inconceivable, overwhelming, ungodly horror. And so I fail, and fail again, and then again, remaining imprisoned inside this paralyzing muteness while the silent and unidentified terror permeates even the humblest and most private regions of my daily life, fear, pain, and terror rising silently and invisibly from every curbstone and every sidewalk crack, from every lamp post and fire hydrant, every alleyway and window, every brick, hallway, latch, and door, every face, every screen, every pair of unseeing, passing, silent eyes.

3

Resistance

The dentist's office I've been going to for half a century has come to seem like a small capsule, a microcosm, of terror. I understand that this is due, in part, to nothing more than the passage of time, but I also know there's more to it than that. At the beginning, back around 1972 or 1973, the dentist who worked on my teeth was the father, a pleasant enough man then in his sixties who remained my dentist until he retired and subsequently died. After that, his son took over, and enough time now has passed so that he, too, has retired, although still alive. My current dentist—one of three now in the practice—is a cousin of the retired son. I trust him as a dentist, although I don't particularly like—or trust—him beyond that. It's no fault of his own, I know, yet also no credit, that he's extremely handsome and a seemingly perfect example, in body type, of the somatotonic mesomorph—tall, muscular, and handsome, a Steve Canyon or a Dick Tracy. Although I'm successful in forcing myself to do it, I don't like looking him in the eye because I simply don't know what might be inside his head. While he talks about pockets and referrals, erosions and cavities and "watch lists," I find myself wondering what kind of thoughts are *really* rattling their cages somewhere behind those suspiciously opaque black eyes and that high granite brow.

A couple of years ago, one of the people who clean teeth—one of the "dental hygienists"—left the practice for greener pastures. She was replaced by someone named Maureen, who has become my confidante, as it were, insofar as she is the only person in the office I trust any more. She's the one who has been the catalyst, in good part, for my fear of the clinic as a microcosm of terror.

Maureen is in her late thirties, I would guess, and she comes from Ireland, county Cork. Her husband still lives there, and the two see one another only certain parts of each year. Four brothers live in Cork as well, as do their aged parents—until recently, that is. The father died sometime within the past four months at the age of 84.

At my most recent appointment, a week or two ago, I asked Maureen, as I always do, how her parents were doing.

"Ah," she said, in her light brogue, "they're okay."

Then I asked, again as I always do, whether she'd traveled home since I'd last been in to see her. Yes, she had. As for her brothers and their families, when I asked about them, she said,

"Ah, they're okay."

Something in her tone was unconvincing, as was something in the lack of detail she was offering. I decided simply to wait for more. And, sure enough, twenty minutes or so later, she paused in her tapping and scraping, took the "saliva ejector" out of my mouth, and explained to me that her father had died since I'd last been in.

"But I'm not telling patients, you see," she told me. "*They* know," she went on, referring with a toss of her head to the receptionists, the other hygienists and assistants, the dentists themselves. "But I'm not telling patients."

Unsure as I was as to what her reasons might be for such a decision, I let it go, expressed my condolences, asked no more.

But I was rewarded for treading lightly, since she soon went on and told me more—her father's age, his prideful and virulent distrust of doctors, his saying that he would follow their orders and then never doing so, his absolute refusal to be sent to an old-age home, and so forth.

I felt privileged at being told things—intimate things—that Maureen kept from other patients. The fact is that we had a bond, not a powerful one, but a bond of some slight but durable type. I think of it, if truth be told, as being a literary bond. As far as I can tell, Maureen is the only one in the clinic who reads.

I know this because of Frank McCourt and *Angela's Ashes*. The first time I saw Maureen for an appointment, I asked what part of Ireland she came from. And it was Cork. I told her that all the way back in the 1960s, in Iowa City, I'd had an instructor named Brian McMahon, a schoolmaster and short story writer from Cork. On top of that, I added, I'd read *Angela's Ashes*.

"Ah, yes. Of course," Maureen whispered. "That's all in Cork."

Never before had I met a dental hygienist who was also a reader. A door opened, maybe not wide, but open. For a bit that day, we talked about books, not much, but some. And there started the bond.

•

Whenever I go to the dentist, I make sure to take along something to read, not only to fill time in the waiting room but also in the dentist's chair, for those spells when the dentist leaves the room and doesn't come back for ten or fifteen minutes. Now and then one or another of the dental assistants will put the question as to what it is I'm reading—and sometimes even Steve Canyon himself will ask—but never with any real interest or any follow-up as to how I like it, what it's about, whether I'd recommend it, and so on. Idle inquiries, in short, made by people who themselves don't read. Or want to.

Except for Maureen, whom I've taken to calling "the secret agent," although admittedly only to myself. Bit by bit, visit by visit, I've learned that Maureen actually thinks about things—maybe doesn't think about much, or about many things, or not deeply, but she does think. All the way back—in her Irish years, childhood, high school, college—she got an education, and she hasn't let it go. She's skeptical. She doesn't take things at face value. She's not, like the others, a passive conformist. And our bond—frail as it may be, it's woven out of something strong—allows us even to mention *politics* without fear. Elections are coming. What do I think of Kathy Hochul? Lee Zeldin? Eric Adams? Maureen admitted to me, her brogue reduced almost to a whisper, that she might not vote this time around.

On my most recent visit, I brought along a handful of articles I'd seen online but hadn't yet read. I'd printed them off and stapled them together.

When Maureen asked what I was reading, I showed her the title of the first article: "Prosecution for COVID Crimes—Discussion Between Francis A. Boyle & Dr. Joseph Mercola." In a few words I explained who Boyle and Mercola were and why they were important. I added that I'd read several books by Boyle and that he had just brought out a new one, which I had ordered and would soon read.

"And what is that one?" she asked me.

I told her it was called *Resisting Medical Tyranny: Why the COVID-19 Mandates Are Criminal* and asked whether she would like me to write it down.

"Oh, no," she said. "I can remember that."

Perhaps she could. I expect so. But when she stepped behind me to make notes and organize the tools she'd been using (we were waiting for Steve Canyon to come in and examine my newly cleaned teeth), I tore off a strip from the bottom of one of my articles and wrote down "Francis A. Boyle" and the title of his new book and then these two others:

Dr. Vernon Coleman, <u>Social Credit: Nightmare on Your Street</u>
Dr. Vernon Coleman, <u>Endgame: The Hidden Agenda 21</u>

When Maureen came back to the side of the dentist's chair, I held out the strip of paper to her.

"Here," I said. "I wrote it down anyway. And two others that I've read. Coleman is excellent."

And then the small, tiny, all but unnoticeable thing happened that made me realize how completely the clinic really had come to feel dangerous, a microcosm of terror.

Maureen took the paper from me and, without so much as a glance at it, slipped it deeply into the side pocket of her white coat and, in the same motion, turned to the supply table as though something there needed attention—all of this in the same instant as the door opened and in walked Steve Canyon.

·

A few years back, the authoritarians began turning up the decibel-level on sirens. First the ambulances were made painfully loud, then the police cars, finally the fire trucks. All of these, also, were converted from mechanical to electronic sirens so that they could—as they do now—make sounds ranging from the painfully shrill, high, and piercing on down to the *WAW*-waw-*WAW*-waw of European ambulances like those in 1930s movies, or even to the brutal impact-sounds of blunt force, repetitive and fast, machine-gun style: **POK POK POK POK POK POK.**

The purpose of these painfully amplified sounds—and the blinding lights that go with them—is not to clear traffic or alert people or to let it be known that an emergency of one kind or another is being responded to by sworn civil guardians.

No, the purpose is to scare and intimidate, put people down, awe them, make them afraid of power. These Brobdingnagian lights and sounds are the tools not of servants but of bullies, and their purpose is to subjugate and weaken the populace, make them pliable, passive, and accepting, so that when the final coup does come, it will come without resistance.

The tools that will follow after these sounds and lights are along the lines of pepper spray and mace, tasers and billy clubs, truncheons, bats, cuffs, guns.

•

For most of my life, as I've mentioned, I have lived in fear of the future and, as a result, I chose to spend my grown years studying, visiting, and nurturing the past. I am now eighty-one years old, and what I most fear now is that the past is slipping away more quickly than ever, inexorably, and that nothing can be done to save or to slow its loss as an ignorant, inhumane, monstrous, cruel future takes over.

I have seen evidence of this, and often, in my mind's eye, I see bits of evidence again. In the night, for example, when sirens flare up and down the avenue in pursuit of the people and of the people's dreams, I see something again: The quick, deft movement of Maureen's hand as she slips the forbidden paper into the side of her white coat and still more quickly turns away.

6

1

Losses

i

If she had lived in an earlier time—the second half of the 19th Century, say—my mother would probably have been declared "neurasthenic." By the time she was born, however—in 1919— that was a word already at the end of its life, falling from the lips of fewer and fewer every year and soon to be forgotten entirely. My mother—even as a very young woman— was thought of instead as being "high-strung" or perhaps, by some, "a nervous case." As a kid under ten or so, like most boys in the tribe of that ungainly age, I had no real impression of my mother that would lead me to make judgment of her. I thought of her as my mother, exactly that: The one who was always there, who fed me, cared for me, tucked me in, woke me up, got me off to school. Not until junior high school did that consciousness begin to change—when, for example, I would invite friends or classmates over and began seeing my mother not by looking at her with my own eyes but by see- ing—and hearing about—the way *my friends* reacted to her and the things *they* said about her. In high school I slowly became better equipped to understand my mother without the help of others, and in college—where for the first time in my life I read *books* about such things and as a result was able to grab, however desperately, onto the bottommost hem of my own adulthood—I began to understand still more. And I know now, these half-dozen decades later, not only that my mother—a birdlike, petite, extremely pretty, very assertive brunette—not only *was* a nervous case, but also that, having come from a torn and badly troubled family of her own, she most certainly *could* have benefitted—abundantly—from psychological counselling, and very possibly as a result could have come to an entirely different end than she did. Yet at the same time she would never in a million years have tolerated the least notion of undergoing such a thing. Inconceivable. No more conceivable than that she would ever have admitted a need for it in the first place.

None whatsoever.

Still, everyone knew the simple truth that my mother was indeed flighty, nervous, and very, very demanding, often uncompromisingly so. It was less clear then, though perfectly clear now, that in her emotional life she was treacherously unbalanced, that she walked a narrow line, that she had a more difficult time playing with a full deck than do most people, for whom psychologically-induced shortcuts of that kind so familiar to my mother don't even arise as a choice.

Whether it was this way with her—psychologically, I mean—from the very beginning, I'm not entirely sure, although I tend to suspect it may well have been so, however much amplified by the death of her father. In a way, it hardly matters, since the underlying story of her life remains the same: My mother went through certain early and destabilizing experiences that instilled in her a powerful, virtually consuming horror of loss, of losing social respectability, of being tainted by even the least appearance of poverty or of anything at all that might carry with it any whisper or hint of the ugly, culpable, or sordid.

The early story is simple but also grievously unpleasant. My mother was born the youngest of three siblings in Red Elm, Illinois, one of the many working-class towns fanning out south and southwestward from Chicago. Her own mother was a homemaker, her father a switchman in the Illinois Central yards. Her two older brothers, as they matured, revealed themselves with increasing reliability to be lazy, unmotivated, and loutish, with an underlying proclivity toward the criminal.

My mother was sixteen when the children's father died and left the family, without its bread earner, exposed to the very real specter of poverty, if not penury. The brothers showed little inclination to be helpful, and as a matter of fact, as if they had grown old ahead of their time—the older was three years out of high school, the other a year—they actually appeared secretly relieved at what seemed an opportunity to distance themselves from the remains of the family and, as it were, to cut free. My mother, on the other hand, instead of going back to high school for her own junior year there, took a job as telephone operator in downtown Red Elm and stayed with that post for the next four years. At the same time as she made that self-limiting decision, her own mother, partly under the questionable influence of her sons, converted the family home into a boarding house. In this rather desperate enterprise, my grandmother served as proprietress, cook, and laundress, while my mother, while continuing at the phone company on a midnight to eight a.m. shift, would sleep each day until four or so in the afternoon, then help with dinner, dishes, and clean-up until it was time for her next shift.

Things continued in that way for a handful of years, all the way into the summer of 1939, with these two women alone, this remnant of a family, managing to scrape their way toward securing a life of at least outward respectability, albeit at the cost of my mother's forfeiture of her high school diploma and any education that might have gone beyond that.

Near this point, the story turned sharply, in fact hideously, for the worse. In the heat of July 1938, late one night, in a bar in Calumet City, the older of the two brothers, the one named Merle, who was by then 24 (to his sister's 19), having gone into a rage at another patron of the bar over money that was owed Merle but that had gone unpaid, fought—and killed—the derelict party. In exactly what way this person was killed, or by what instrument or tool, I don't know. How large an amount of money was in question, I don't know. For what purpose the money had originally been loaned, I don't know either, nor do I know by what means or in what way Merle had first come into possession of it.

I know only that the dreadful incident did occur. And I know that in the autumn of 1938, Merle was tried, convicted, and sentenced by the court to forty-five years confinement in Joliet Prison.

I know so little as this for the obvious reason that those who *did* know were also those most desirous of seeming, or even pretending, *not* to know. They were the most desirous that others *not* know. And they were the most passionate of anyone anywhere in wishing that things be arranged in such a way that that long-ago murder on a hot summer night in a Calumet City bar had never happened, taken place, so much as existed.

ii

One afternoon near the end of May 1940, the young man who was to become my father walked up to the boarding house door and knocked. When my grandmother answered, he told her that he was looking for room and board for an indefinite length of time. He would be able to pay, he told her, by the week, in advance.

That was how my parents met. The two of them courted

through the following summer and into the fall, all the way up to Thanksgiving. They got married on the first of December, and my sister, Zoë, was born on June 15th of the following year. I myself had to wait until February of 1947 to come into existence. In my case the name they—my mother—chose was Julian.

iii

My father was born and raised in the town of St. James, Missouri, but when he and my mother met he had come north and taken a job in one of the oil refineries just across the Illinois-Indiana state line. As things worked out, he never did return to Missouri but remained for good in the area south and southwest of Chicago, where my sister and I were born and raised.

Our father was honest, good-enough looking, and both steadfast and extremely hard-working. He possessed, however, very little—almost nothing—in the way of imagination.

That deficiency in him was something our mother pretended to be frustrated, even exasperated, by, but in later decades I came to understand that in fact it suited her perfectly.

After all, what my mother wanted to do above anything else was to fashion her life in such a way that she could live it in total and absolute hiding—in hiding from the past, from poverty, from failure and criminality, from anything tainted in the least way whatsoever by the poor, wretched, sordid, low, or criminal.

In a word, my mother wanted to be *respectable*. And the best—perhaps the only—way for her to achieve that state, or that appearance, was for her to hide from the past as completely and as absolutely as she possibly could.

When I was young—in kindergarten, grade school, junior high—I didn't, as I said earlier, think about things of this kind at all, about my parents, wondering who they *were*, and certainly not about my mother. Only later did I begin to learn or see enough to understand just how fragile or unstable her life really was, or just how strong the fears and desires were that drove her to create around us, never allowing it to lapse, a life that had every outward appearance of being comfortable and well off, a life perfect and orderly, impeccable in every last detail.

My father, without his so much as knowing it, was the ideal participant in my mother's plan. His own childhood had been, unlike my mother's, a happy one, or certainly happy enough that he commonly reflected back on it in the years of Zoë's and my growing up. He was the middle in a family of three children, and his own father was a tradesman well enough liked and known in town to have been elected mayor of St. James for a four-year term that began in 1932, when my father was thirteen. I said of him earlier that he had little or no imagination, and that was true, but he had an overwhelming supply of manual skill, perseverance, and willingness to work. The summer after ninth grade he began apprenticing for his father, learning how to do pipe-fitting and plumbing installations. The next year, during tenth grade, he began also putting in two or three hours after school, leaving his homework to be done when dinner was over. Things went on this way through tenth, eleventh, then twelfth grades, and by the time he received his high school diploma he was also possessor of his plumber's license. By this time it was 1937. Toward fall of that year he took some of his earnings and bought a used Model Y Ford and set out for Alton, Illinois, to look for—and get—work on the river dam being built there. It was completed at the end of 1938, but before the project ended my father had had the foresight to seek out someone to teach him welding, so that by the time he left Alton he was not only a plumber and pipe-fitter but also a welder. These were skills enough to draw him farther north, and he headed for the refineries on

Lake Michigan just across the Illinois-Indiana line. He was hired there as an "oiler" and for three or four months lived in a room in a shabby hotel close to work, while keeping his eye open for something better. He was making more money than he'd made at Alton, and, thinking he would prefer living on the Illinois side of the border instead of the Indiana side, he now and then drove over there to look around. One night he ended up at a bar in Blue Island, where he found himself sitting next to a sullen but friendly enough young man who said his name was Sam Handke. The two fell into conversation and at one point Sam Handke suggested that if my father was looking for a place to live he should look at Sam's mother's boarding house in Red Elm. That was how it happened that my parents first met one another and how it was—a few months later for Zoë and six years later for me—that my sister and I came into existence.

For better or for worse.

iv

From the beginning, my father earned a generous amount of money in the refineries, but after the end of World War II (assuming for the moment that it ever did end), he took home even better pay. By the time I came along, in 1947, he had been promoted from the rank of worker up to that of crew foreman, then beyond that to what they called floor foreman. Then, when I had reached six years of age—and Zoë had reached twelve—he set aside his working clothes and switched into the neckties and jackets, the pressed pants and shined shoes of those who had desks and offices and were in "planning and management."

My father was never an "oil executive," or at least I never thought of him as one, and I very much doubt that he did either. He was something closer to a job-overseer or a workers' manager. Certainly he had the experience for it. He himself had started out by working with his hands—for pay—at thirteen or fourteen, and now, after almost two and a half decades of being a workman, he became a manager.

As far as I was able to tell, it never changed him in any real way. He came home from work in different clothes than before, but he changed out of them the same as ever—except that now, instead of spending the evening in a tee shirt, he would spend it in a sport shirt or a white shirt with the sleeves rolled up. He still opened a beer and sat at the kitchen table talking with my mother as she fixed dinner, then took a second beer into the living room to read the paper or, later, to watch the news on television.

His habits and interests didn't change. He still followed his favorite teams when they were in season, and he still liked cars and watching them race. During the stock car season—from late spring to halfway through the summer—he would still take me on weekends to the Illini/Red Elm track half a mile from where we lived to watch some of the races. That was where I became aware of Bud Ackerman, someone who plays an important part in the story I'm now telling, even though (if I were to tell the truth), I'm not certain I know what it's really about.

Bud Ackerman became something of a hero to me at the time. He was soft-spoken and pleasant, always very polite. He worked on his own in a one-man business as painter, contractor, and repairman, and he had a son close to my own age, a fact that made him a little bit more attentive to me than he might have otherwise been, asking me, for example, what grade I was in at one given time or another and remarking that his son was in the same grade. I knew his son but only slightly and wasn't friends with him. The Ackerman family lived all the way across town on the far side of Red Elm, and they were Catholic on top of it, so that Patrick went to a different school than I did.

Not only was Bud one of the two or three top drivers at the track, but he had also been a flyer, had flown in the

Korean war, and was missing the first finger on his right hand. The day he came over to our house to do some painting for my mother—the day of the accident I hope to tell about—I watched him at work for a while at the beginning of the job and marveled at how well he handled a paint brush even with that missing finger.

At the track he drove a Studebaker Sky Hawk painted pure black, and almost always he was the first one going into the turns, and almost always the fastest racer, partly because his car had a lower center of gravity than most of the others—although also because he was a wonderful driver.

On quiet and still summer evenings, from our house, you could hear the sounds from the racetrack low and in the distance.

•

My father never understood—or cared to know, for that matter—just how my mother was using him in her project of hiding from the past. It wasn't in his nature to wonder about it, really. My father was simply the good husband, the one whose role it was to generate the means whereby comfort and well-being could be provided for the family—and at that point his responsibility—and I suspect also his *interest*—came more or less to an end. Zoë and I, certainly, weren't about to make determinations about household expenditures or decide which styles of design or décor or even architecture were appropriate or suitable for the family. All of these matters therefore remained the prerogative of my mother, who seized on them with an almost grim delight and with a driving lust for perfection, a drive that for the most part she disguised as being nothing more, really, than the exercise of good taste and a perfectly normal desire for an orderly home.

Insofar as that disguise could be kept in place—the disguise that all things regarding our family were normal and that all things were impeccably respectable and permanent—with that disguise in place, my mother believed she could hold her own in the battle to keep the past from rising again, from coming back with a vengeance to claim her.

In our house, therefore, nothing was ever out of place, indoors or out, and nothing was tacky, tawdry, worn out, or smudged. The house itself was good-looking, on the large side, and many-windowed. High-roofed, it was sided with white clapboard and it offered four rooms on the ground floor (as well as a very wide front porch) and four more on the second, not to mention an attic above and a finished basement below. Nothing in my mother's house went unnoticed and nothing went unattended. The interior was airy, and every window was fitted either with draperies or with simple curtains of a pattern and color suitable to the room they hung in. The living room itself was spacious, thickly carpeted in wall-to-wall beige and sporting a large sectional sofa shaped like the letter "L," as well, of course, as other furniture. The carpet was never unvacuumed, no exposed wood was ever unpolished, no drapery ever uncleaned. No ashtray retained for long any signs of the use for which it was intended. The glass one on the side table beside my father's reading chair would hold at least three or four stubs when he stood up to come to dinner. And yet after the meal, even before dishes were done, it would have been swapped for a clean and shiny replacement. In the kitchen, my mother was, if anything, even more quick, orderly, and fastidious than she was elsewhere in the house. Only seldom was anyone else in the family invited or allowed—including Zoë—to assist in the preparing or serving of meals, or even to help in the cleanup. My mother, in the eyes of some, might have been considered a dervish or a compulsive, and in a certain number of ways, perhaps—no, not *perhaps*—she was. Just as she was considered "high-strung" by others, she was also in the faintest way slightly mad in her compulsion for things to be invariably and exactly in their places and for tasks to be done in precisely the way she wanted them done. Other people, however well intended, were in my mother's view likely to be more hindrance than help, considering the many tiny errors and missteps that they were certain to make.

My mother's need was in parts both intense and deep, her fighting of a war to keep the past at bay—or, more accurately, a war to keep the past *down*, her foot dug firmly into its recumbent neck so that it could never again raise its incorrigibly ugly head.

For a war of this kind to be waged properly, it was necessary that it be waged alone, by only the best prepared and best equipped, and by only the most committed, motivated, dedicated, and inspired.

My mother knew with perfect certainty who that was.

How lonely she must have been, how terribly lonely, until she simply couldn't stand it any longer.

V

It's necessary for me to introduce the subject of my friendship with Tom Germundson.

The day I'm finding a way to tell about is a day in late spring of the year I had just finished sixth grade. That I'd completed sixth grade meant that Zoë had completed twelfth at the same time, and in the fall of that year she was to leave home and go off to New College, in West Tree, Minnesota.

The exact date was Friday, June 5th, 1959. The day of More Losses, as I think of it now.

•

My friendship with Tom was a close one, while it lasted, though it didn't reach very far back. Not long past the spring break in my fifth-grade year, Tom appeared as a new kid in class. His family had just moved to Red Elm from Columbia,

Missouri, and in fact had moved into a house not at all far from my own. Most of the blocks in our part of town still had alleyways running through them, vestiges of the days when people needed access to the stables that, invariably, were situated at the rear of their properties. Our own block had such an alley. Now, the house my family lived in was situated on the southeast corner of the block, while Tom's was one house in from the northwest corner of the same block. If either of us wanted to visit the other, we didn't need to cross a street or even use a sidewalk. All we had to do was run along the alley one way or the other through the block and then cross through the other person's backyard to their house.

In our section of fifth grade, the teacher had us sit alphabetically, and when Tom arrived she made the necessary seat changes in order to keep the alphabetical order. So it came about, Tom's last name being Germundson and mine being Handke, that his new spot was right in front of mine. It was perfectly natural that I would get to know him.

Jim was one of the nicest kids I ever knew, or ever was to know. I have no idea how smart he really was—not very, I don't think, although I was to know him for only a year and a couple of months, hardly a long time for sixth-graders to get to know one another intellectually, or even to think very much about smartness. In any case, Tom's mildness of manner and his companionability, his good nature generally, were tremendously attractive and made his company a pleasure. Every now and then, we would have a "library period" at school when the teacher would take the whole class to the "library"—just another classroom except that books and periodicals were shelved along its walls and the floor space was filled with five or six reading tables, each surrounded by half a dozen chairs. I liked the library period, and Tom and I fell into the habit of seeking out a handful of magazines or illustrated books featuring airplanes, cars, or heavy equipment of one kind or another. These we would take to a reading table and sit side by side as we paged slowly through them, each of us, in a voice nearly inaudible, going "ooooh" when we saw an especially impressive picture of a bulldozer, airplane, locomotive, or an oversized truck, with its elephantine wheels, offloading broken rock over a cliff's edge. It may be that I never had time to find out whether Tom was ahead of me in school-learning ways, or behind, or beside me, but he was far ahead when it came to mechanical things and using his hands. From his bedroom ceiling there hung, on strings of varying lengths, what must have been eight or ten model airplanes of different types and sizes, from early biplanes on through a DC-3 and even a Lockheed Constellation. Every one of them was shapely and flawless, and every one was impeccably painted. I admired them immensely, even after Tom, being nothing if not candid, told me—the first time I saw his room—that he hadn't built them by himself but only with his father's help. Even then the achievement seemed impressive to me, and I was envious of it. For that matter, I remember being envious of Tom's father himself, or, more accurately, envious of Tom's having *him* for a father. Tall, lean, and quite good-looking, he was a professor of geology at the Joliet School of Mining and wore dashing tweed jackets or, in hot weather, white shirts with the sleeves rolled above the elbows. And although the family car was nothing but a four-door Chevrolet, he himself drove his own MG-TD, a dashing and sporty little car with spoke wheels and a body painted in a deep racing green, a car that, if I'm to be absolutely honest, was another thing to make me jealous. Tom's father, who had a reputation for speeding, invariably drove the TD with the top down whenever the weather was fair, and I could hardly have been more envious of Tom than on those occasions when I would see him riding around in it with his father at the wheel.

Of course, that was also the car that ushered them through the veil and out of existence.

•

I suppose now I have to come to the thing itself, the new loss. Where it happened was on County Highway 3. This at one time was just a gravel road, but a number of years back it had been widened and macadamized so as to serve as a connector between Red Elm and the new expressway, lying five miles or so east of town, that went north into Chicago and south toward St. Louis.

I don't know what it's like now, sixty-plus years later, but in Tom's and my time it was still just a lightly used highway running through open countryside and farmland, with almost no build-up other than the usual farm houses and homesteads, with their groves, barns, silos, livestock, systems of fencing, and so on.

The one exception was the rock quarry, which lay on the north side of the road more or less halfway between Red Elm and the Interstate.

The quarry looked as if an immense bowl had been dug out of the earth, its perimeter at ground level necessarily growing wider and wider as the pit itself went down ever deeper. By the time Tom and I were aware of the quarry and had formed the habit of riding our bikes out to visit it, the rim must have measured a third of a mile across. How far down the pit itself actually went, I can't really imagine, but it gave an impression of almost unimaginable depth. The huge pieces of heavy machinery at work in the bottom, with their claws, treads, jaws, drills, and crushers, all appeared immensely diminished by distance. Tom and I looked down at them from the rim, where we would sit at one or another of the perches we sought out with great care. In order for us to consider a perch successful, it had to be unquestionably solid and firm, but it also had to be such that we could hang our legs down from the knees, while at the same time it had to provide grass for us to sit on. And, of course, it was essential that it provide us with a panoramic and unobstructed view.

Over time, the project had been excavated in such a way that the sides of the huge bowl were terraced with roads spiraling their way down to the bottom of the pit. The immense trucks with their huge oversized tires and open beds—empty—would make their way around and around the circumference, descending slowly in one of their lowest gears, until they reached the bottom and could be loaded up before beginning their ascent. Sometimes they made their slow, engine-roaring and exhaust-belching climbs loaded just with dirt, although at other times their beds would be filled with rock, either crushed or in huge jagged pieces that gleamed white in the sunshine.

Just as we had done back in the school library, Tom and I from time to time would emit our low exclamations of "ooooh," especially when we happened to be witness to an episode of blasting. You could tell when a blast was going to take place because all movement would gradually come to a halt. The spiral roadways would slowly become empty of trucks, which would either wait up at the top or park and wait down in the bottom. The roar and grind of the heavy machines down there would come to a stop one by one, and for a minute or two there would be a strange, unfamiliar, pleasant silence. Then the whistle—where it came from, exactly, I could never find out—would give out its three short and shrill sounds of warning. And after a minute's delay—it seemed immensely long—we would hear a small and distant yet powerful sound, a muffled *thud* that always made me think of a huge safe, or a bank vault—thoroughly wrapped up in thick movers' quilts—being dropped through the floor of one immense room down onto the marble floor of the next.

·

It would be as if nothing had happened. The muffled sound came and went, admittedly, but otherwise it would seem as if nothing had happened. No change was made that your eyes could detect. Afterward, there was an immense quietness for a minute or two. Then the whistle would blow the all clear, and the trucks and machines would start up their engines, bringing sound everywhere again, and then movement.

vi

How it happened, or why, I don't know. But someone traveling from east to west managed to go off the shoulder on the long curve the highway made around the south and southwest lip of the rock quarry. Whoever it was, they were able to bring their car to a stop just before it went far enough to plunge down into the yawning pit. In the end, the right front wheel hung just over the edge, while the back left hung in the air six inches off the ground. Perfect balance. The driver opened the door, stepped out, and walked away.

This happened after midnight, somewhere in the very small hours. Next morning sometime between ten and eleven the wrecker came, supposedly with a crew of three men. Two of these, carrying red flags, were to walk along the highway, one east and one west, until they disappeared well out of sight around the long blind curve. There, they were to take up posts allowing them to flag down any approaching cars and bring them to a stop. The third man, meanwhile, positioned the wrecker on the far side of the highway, faced away from the open quarry. He unspooled a cable from the wrecker's winch mechanism, drew it across the highway, and affixed it to a tow-point under the rear chassis of the car in jeopardy. He then returned to the wrecker's rear end and, working the levers of the winch mechanism, gradually tightened up the tow-cable. The terrain was such that, as it tightened, the cable rose up three feet or so above the surface of the highway. As the tow-operator increased the tension on the cable even more, the endangered car at last began to move back from the lip of the quarry, not even an inch at first, but then two, maybe three. At exactly that moment Tom and his father appeared around the long curve in the green MG-TD, coming at a very high speed. It's unlikely that they ever saw the cable at all, which was at just the right height, as the little car passed under it, to shear off the raked windshield and to do the same also to both of their heads.

vii

As you can imagine, this isn't something I've forgotten, even though I never saw it with my own eyes. As a kid of twelve, once I'd finally been allowed to hear enough detail to figure out for myself what had happened, the imagined version I had of the horror was remarkably primitive, simple, and unadorned. In my mind's eye I saw the car, and the cable, then two heads rising upward suddenly and quite neatly. And that was that, more or less. I didn't think to wonder where the heads *went* after that, or where the *car* went, for that matter, whether it remained upright or rolled over, or perhaps flew down into the pit, and whether it remained a container for the two headless bodies, or whether it flung them out of itself as if desiring to be purged of its ruined cargo.

I'm now seventy-six years old, however, and I've had plenty of time to think, you might say, more questioningly about the accident. By no means does it come to my mind—and by no means *has* it come to my mind—either regularly or obsessively over these decades, but something happened not long ago that brought it back to my mind and that has kept it there lately in a more or less stubborn way, if you will.

What happened was a very simple thing, really. A little over three years ago now, I made a trip to New York City for a few days' visit with my sister Zoë and her husband, the writer Malcolm Reiner. Zoë was ill at the time and in fact passed away not very long after my visit, at the age of seventy-eight. Still, as almost always happened on our reunions, she and I fell into nostalgic and rather wide-ranging reminiscences about Red Elm, about our parents (both by then departed, mother long before father), about our childhoods—in short, about the past. And, for reasons I don't entirely remember, I found myself reminiscing about Tom Germundson. I suspect it may have begun with my drifting back to memories of Tom's collection of model airplanes, and from there, undoubtedly, to the memory of his father's MG-TD—and then, inevitably enough, to the accident, and along the way recollections of Bud Ackerman, the stock car track, Zoë's summer math classes, our mother...

The significant thing for me was that the longer I went on with my recollections, the more visibly fascinated my brother-in-law became. He leaned forward in his chair, elbows on knees. He asked questions. He got up and went over to his desk, came back with a yellow legal pad, sat down again. He began making *notes*.

There's meaning in all this, he said. Intricate, in its own way profound.

I told him that he ought to write it up; he was the one to do it, not me; *he* was the writer.

And I think he may actually have begun working on it. But then later that summer Zoë's illness worsened and she passed away in late August of 2019. After that, I don't know how much writing Malcolm continued to do. He and I drifted apart, albeit slowly. I hadn't seen him for almost three years after Zoë's death. And now he's gone too.

But, oddly enough, the "story" has stayed with me. I haven't been able to stop wondering about the "meaning" that Malcolm was so certain about, if only you could find it.

I'm not so sure. Although it does seem to consist, in one way or another, of layers upon layers...

It's no secret that I've tried here to write it myself. And it's also no secret that I've wandered all over the map trying to tie together the elusive "meaning" that Malcolm was so certain about. Look at me, going back to 1935, all the way back to the boarding house, my grandfather's death and then the late-night murder in Calumet City—in an effort to explain my mother's all-absorbing need to bury the past by painting the present in lovely colors—all this in my own attempt to find the "meaning" in a story triggered by an accident that grew only more horrible and again more so the more I thought about it, let myself "see" it, so that it wasn't just two heads rising upward suddenly and quite neatly, but two heads bouncing along the highway like flung and broken melons, two up-gushers of blood from the blind necks still sitting in the bucket seats of the trim and sporty little MG-TD that I once so coveted...

viii

As for meaning. When it happened, each of us was busy in our own way, totally unaware of the moment when Tom and his father raced toward, and then plunged into, the tautened cable.

Friday, June 5th, 1959. A day perfect, impeccable, sun-filled, warm, calm.

Between ten o'clock and eleven in the morning. My father was in Chicago, twenty-three miles away from Red Elm, at his desk at Beckham, Oliver, & Sterne, Inc. Four days earlier, Zoë had begun summer classes at Southwest Community, and now she sat out on the front porch, on the shady side of the house, barefoot, on the chain swing, her legs curled under her, at work on calculus problems. Inside the house, Bud Ackerman, first finger missing on his right hand, was setting himself up to put a fresh coat of white paint on our staircase. Wearing knee pads, he knelt on the top step so as to make his way down gradually as he painted stairs, posts, newels, banister. My mother, as usual, wore a one-piece house dress with a wide hem that fell just below her knees, was drawn tight at the waist, and had short puff-sleeves. Mostly she spent time in the kitchen. Now and then I could hear the sounds of crockery or of saucepans being placed on a burner. From time to time, my mother went out to the bottom of the stairs and asked Bud Ackerman if there were anything he needed. She was baking cookies. I also caught the scent of fresh coffee. From the kitchen, my mother took a plate of the cookies and a cup of the coffee to Bud Ackerman, insisted he take a break, and for a time sat on one of the lower steps talking with him. She took some cookies also out to the porch for Zoë. At one point she called out to me from the back door, asking if I would like to come in for some of my own.

As for me, I was out on the driveway practicing softball pitches. With black electrician's tape I had marked off a square on the closed garage door indicating what I considered to be the strike zone. Then, standing at the bottom of the driveway, I would throw my pitch, listen to the *thud* against the door, retrieve the ball, return to the bottom of the drive, and throw again.

As I said, the day was warm, lovely, calm, still. And the sound of my ball against the garage door seems to me now to have been like the sound of a heartbeat, an extremely slow one, the heartbeat, perhaps, of some antediluvian creature dropping slowly toward silence, extinction, and death.

•

Each of us was separate. One from another. No knowing. No touching. No helping.

All these years later, it is only the more so. I am resigned never to know what Malcolm saw in it. If he did. What I myself fear is that the meaning in it is no meaning.

As if not even echoes exist any more.

2

The Unspeakable

1

For the longest time, I didn't think Jonathan Fried was mad, but just very, very stubborn. Now, though, with real pity and sorrow, I think he's nutty as a fruitcake. I think his head is a barn full of swallows.

Without any doubt, Jonathan is one of the smartest people I've ever met. When he was in eighth grade he tested into Stuyvesant High School and not only went there instead of staying in his Queens neighborhood but graduated co-valedictorian and went off to Yale on a National Merit Scholarship that covered tuition, books, housing, everything. First major: mathematics. Second major: comparative literature. Graduation: 1978.

I met him eleven years ago, in 2011, when he and his extremely beautiful love-companion, Regina, had just moved into the building I myself had lived in for decades. Location of that first meeting: entrance lobby. Cast of characters: building tenants. Subject: bedbugs. Main action: my mentioning "diatomaceous earth" as being useful in helping keep bedbugs away.

I dislike affectation, in speech particularly, and have always taken pains to avoid it. But there was something in the syllabic melody of "diatomaceous earth" when I spoke those words that caught Jonathan's attention. A couple of days later, as my wife and I were coming into the building, Jonathan happened to be coming out of it. He looked down at me—Jonathan is six-five; I am much less—as if he were Darwin scrutinizing a new specimen of plant or some such thing, and asked,

"Are you an academic, by any chance?"

I *was* one of that breed, and so I pled guilty, although, in a nod toward vindication of some slight kind, I added that I'd already for half a decade been retired from the vice of "teaching."

None of that mattered. Once again, Jonathan had spotted—he had sniffed out—another like himself: Another reader, thinker, introvert; another intellectual kin; yet another person who, like him, used books and words, thoughts and reading, to examine, and then to re-examine still more deeply, what it meant to be at once a physical and a psychological being, what it meant to have awareness, empathy, consciousness, what it meant to be alive and what it meant—*Hamlet* was a favorite referent—to face nothingness and yet carve out or create meaning from it, and after that how to protect, preserve, and share it with your fellow beings, since it—*meaning*—was the sole thing that could nourish, enrich, dignify, and make complete the human individual, the human race, the human culture.

·

The business of knowing Jonathan was not a thing that could be taken lightly, and to be a friend with him was not just to be a friend, but to be an *intellectual* friend. Jonathan existed for the purpose of *thinking*, and he did his thinking for the purpose—in any way possible—of rescuing the human species from the thousand degradations and depravities that assailed it from all sides; and then, having rescued it, to go on with the project of creating and maintaining the health and fitness of humanity, the project of strengthening it, ennobling it, making it capable of an ongoing self-sufficiency, this curious organism that was simultaneously biological and cultural, thereby capable—if only it would—of maintaining its own health, its own creativity, its own integrity, its own morality, creating nothing less than its own reasons for continuing to exist, and for doing so in the best possible way and for the best possible ends.

·

For the better part of a decade we met every couple of weeks, or every ten days, even once a week, mostly in Lenny's Bagels at 98th and Broadway. I loved it there—I still do—with its authentic world-class décor of "plain and shabby," its big plate-glass windows on two sides that allowed you to watch the traffic and pedestrians going by, and its disorganized scattering of small tables.

In fact, by remembering Lenny's I can mark the moment when I knew once and for all that the split in our friendship was inevitable.

With the onset of the infamous and nefarious "covid" plague and its ensuing and treacherous "lockdown," our meetings had become gradually less frequent, then still more so, until we met sometimes once a month, sometimes less, then even less than that. From my own eager reading in the "alternative media," I was entirely convinced, by, say, the time mid-summer of 2020 had come around, that the entire health "scare" was based on shameless lies and vicious deceit and was in fact an enormous terrorist plot planned and orchestrated by extraordinarily wealthy, ruthless, and powerfully organized enemies of the people. I spent most of my time throughout the middle and end of 2020, in fact, working feverishly on a book on the subject. I called it *Doom in Slow Motion: A Writer's Notebook from the Years of the Great Covid-19 Terrorism and Genocide Campaign*, and I can now, after not having touched it for well more than a year, admit that its fervent pitch overall may indeed eclipse the few thoughtful, Solonic, reasoned passages that, in my fear, outrage, and disbelief, I was able to summon up.

For most of a year, in any case, the merciless—and mercilessly named—"lockdown" eliminated Lenny's as a meeting place for us, and Jonathan and I saw one another much less frequently than before. Then on top of that, and far more important, another obstacle began to stand in the way of our meeting. This was not a physical obstacle but an intellectual one. To my amazement—and disbelief—it became gradually more and more clear that Jonathan was taking the entire "pandemic" at face value, unskeptically, and with absolute seriousness.

I was unable to believe what I was hearing and seeing. In short, Jonathan was falling for the great lie. Jonathan Fried, the possessor of so extraordinary an intellect; a person who stood as an unwavering model of the will to do good and oppose harm; a man of wide and deep reading, of scientific depth and years of mathematical study—*this* person was falling for the cheapest and most explicit (although at the same time the most massive) program of terror and propaganda to have been visited upon a people since the Nazi subjugation of the German population in the 1930s.

I could try to reconstruct the "stages" of our failing relationship as 2020 crept forward from its "all-lies-all-the-time" terror-debut in mid-March through the perfectly planned denouement of its dread terminus in December, when people began pushing their way by the millions into drug stores, church basements, doctors' offices, and—not least—canvas street-corner tents to get shots of the "vaccine" that they were told would protect them from contracting the deadly virus but that in fact was designed to alter their immune systems forever, beginning the slow but certain process of culling individuals out of the "herd" for all time.

But what would be the point of such a reconstruction of how things went between Jonathan and me, the point of providing a chronicle, scene by scene, step by step, one day after another? No, there'd be no point in that, because the real and honest truth is this: The real and honest truth is that *nothing happened.* The truth is that during 2020 and on through 2021, as I myself read more and more articles, books, and reports; as I slowly pushed forward further and further with "Doom in Slow Motion"; as I listened to speeches and watched videos, as I followed up on one leader, spokesman, dissident, author, journalist after another—as I did all of these things, Jonathan remained absolutely unreceptive to it all, imperturbable, unchanging.

I should have seen it then. Perhaps I *did* see it then.

Yes, of course I did, but only faintly. We'd been to the park, having planned to sit on a bench and talk when the rain began, causing us to walk back up to Broadway. June 2021. There we were, on the sidewalk, outside Lenny's. Mist falling from the sky and growing heavier. Yet, in spite of the rain, Jonathan *still would not go inside.*

That apologetic, hopeless, sorrow-filled look he gets on his face, as if he feels remorse for what he's doing—or is not doing—but also that he is in the grip of a larger force of some kind and *can't* choose otherwise. But for me it was the final straw. All I wanted was to go inside, sit together at a table by a window, nurse a hot coffee, and talk about literature, books—his and mine included—politics, terror, what hope a person could hold for a future...

After that I didn't lay eyes on Jonathan for over a year and a half. Nineteen months. I didn't see him, in fact, until the party for Barbara's seventieth birthday. Just one week ago, November 19, 2022. Jonathan came as a guest and stayed hardly half an hour. I talked with him, though not much. But I saw it then, with withering clarity and great horror, exactly what he was doing.

2

I never knew a time when Jonathan wasn't either reading or writing—or, in point of fact, doing both. In the first three years or so of our decade-long friendship, he produced two volumes of extraordinarily energetic and expressive poetry as well as a short novel that had even greater insight and energy than the poems did, not to mention even greater humor. I published these three books under the aegis of the small press I'd set up a few years after I retired, in despair at the depths that commercial publishing had sunk to and knowing that it would never again publish—I mention solely for example—my own writing, let alone Jonathan's. Jonathan's second book of poems came out in 2012, the short novel in 2014. After that, in what remained of our decade together, we talked Jonathan's magnum opus into existence (or so I like to think we did, and so Jonathan has said).

Or if not into existence, then into the beginning of existence.

Back when he was just out of Yale, when he hadn't yet met and fallen in love with Regina and was in an unrelenting fight against depression—in the early 1980s—Jonathan signed up for a weeklong fiction-writing seminar to be taught by the writer K. O. May and to be held in Poughkeepsie, on the Vassar campus. I knew nothing about this until almost thirty years after the event, when May died—in 2019—after a long and degenerative illness. Before that sad event, I had seen Jonathan's name mentioned with gratitude in May's foreword to his last novel, and during our friendship I learned a good deal, naturally enough, about Jonathan's relationship with this distinguished mentor. In the Vassar seminar, Jonathan's writing had emerged from the crowd and gotten more attention than the other students', but there was something further that Jonathan (and I, certainly) didn't learn about until at least a year after May's death. His widow, Beth Anne, set out bravely on the enormous project of putting her husband's papers in order, and a year or so after his death she sent something remarkable to Jonathan. May had apparently kept diaries about his seminars and the students in them when he was teaching, and Beth Anne came upon an entry about Jonathan from the Vassar seminar. May had written, "Without question, as a genius, Jonathan Fried stands out from the others. I must go on doing what I can to protect him."

•

I have no reason whatsoever to doubt K. O. May's assessment, but at the same time I have never been more uncertain than I am now as to what it might really mean, this "being a genius" thing. Through the long years of our "talking friendship," I was never in the least doubt as to the richness and depth of Jonathan's mind, *and* the richness and depth of his memory. This was especially true in the middle-to-late years of our friendship, those including not only the years when we first actually *talked* the idea of Jonathan's novel into existence, the gestation years, but the following ones too, when Jonathan actually began *writing* it into physical form, shaping, reshaping, altering, expanding, introducing new characters when they might help shed light on the central consciousness of the book. It was an extraordinary thing, huge, ambitious, roomy and capacious, intricate in concept but at the same time transparent, easy-moving, and limber in its structure. Testament not only to its subject but also to its great ambition, it gained between us the working title of "The Institution."

I never laid eyes on so much as a word of it.

And, now, I doubt that I ever will.

I don't say such things spitefully, or as a way of being cutting or snide, as some might do if they wanted to suggest that Jonathan, all along, had just been *claiming* he was hard at work on the book but hadn't actually been *writing*, that everything about it was all talk and no real work.

That's absurd. I can't say that I know for a *fact* that he was working on the book all those many months, but it would be a real trespass on our friendship for me even to think such a thing. He and I, as I said, *talked* the book into existence, and each time we met, the talk went further, the ideas moved forward, and everything about the project became more fully realized, more fully constructed, more compellingly imagined. What I learned about the book in our conversations made me look forward very, very much to reading it on the page, but Jonathan was committed to the idea—at *that* point, he was committed to the idea—that it was essential for him to get it—the whole project—through a completed first draft before he would feel confident in offering it for anyone to read, even if that anyone happened to be me.

No. I'm absolutely certain that he was actively working on the book. And besides that, I'm absolutely certain that he was working *hard*.

How and why this changed, I don't know. Not exactly.

But I know that it means nothing good. I know it means nothing that isn't positively ruinous. Even horrifying.

•

All of this is impossible to believe. All of this is intolerable. *"Without question, as a genius, Jonathan Fried stands out clearly from the others. I must go on doing what I can to protect him."*

Sorrow. Regret. Disbelief.

After his inspiring experience at the prose seminar in

Poughkeepsie, two extremely important things happened to Jonathan. He was at this time twenty-two years old, just recently out of Yale, and living... ? Well, where if not back with his parents, in his old childhood room, in the same Queens apartment where every one of the previous years of his life had passed.

The first of the two incalculably important things that happened after the seminar was so very small—on the surface, that is—that to a casual onlooker it might have seemed as though nothing whatsoever had taken place.

It was this: Jonathan, standing in the kitchen, told his father about the seminar and how things had gone during it, not only that his own work had gained greater interest among the other students than anyone else's, but also that it had gained greater interest—and praise—from the instructor than anyone else's.

That was step one in this incalculably important first of two events. The second step was this: The fact that Jonathan's father responded without congratulatory gesture or word; without warmth of any kind; and without any indication of pride at what his son had accomplished.

Instead, his father said, in no more words than these, turning away,

"I see. Nothing like that ever happened to *me*."

•

The second of the incalculably important things that happened to Jonathan after the seminar in Poughkeepsie was that he stopped writing. He quit absolutely. For twenty years he wrote nothing. And he stayed completely out of touch with K. O. May.

These were the dark years of Jonathan's life. He went on living—that is, he ate, slept, and read—in his childhood room. To support himself, he commuted into the city for jobs—"positions," they were called—as a mathematician and computer programmer for Wall Street investment banks and corporations. At these places, even though he was far better equipped for doing this kind of work than were most of his competitors, the work itself left him panting in emptiness, and as a consequence he moved from job to job with much more frequency than was looked upon with favor. For Jonathan, it became a slow downward spiral professionally—if that's the right word—as it was also a slow downward spiral emotionally. Years later, Jonathan told me that by the time he graduated from Yale, mathematics as something to *practice* had gone dead for him, certainly in any computational sense he could possibly think of. Conceiving of it as a way of modeling future financial or monetary behavior came to seem to him no more meaningful—or enticing—than a basket of dry bones, while at the same time the *philosophy* of mathematics, the epistemology, maybe even the metaphysics of it, if I'm even using the right words—these never faded in interest for him, and in fact around the time when I first met him, a few years before K. O. May's death, he was working on a massive project that, when asked, he would describe simply as "a history of mathematics," though allow me to interject here that, drawing on the many and deep conversations he and I had in the good years of our friendship, it seemed to me far more than simply a "history." In any case, the "dark years" Jonathan suffered through might easily have destroyed a lesser—or a less focused—person, although exactly what Jonathan was focused *on* remained an unanswered question, at least for me. One time around the middle of our friendship, Regina and Jonathan happened to be going through a rough patch in their long love affair, and I remember Regina tossing out at Jonathan something she intended as a barb, saying, with more than a tablespoon or two of acid in her voice—

"With you, everything is just psychology, psychology, psychology all the time, isn't it"—and I must admit she was right, or she was right *if* by "psychology" she meant something deep enough, broad enough, universal enough in its range and scope not only to include all humanity but also to hold the interest of so broad and *continuous* a thinker as her lover. Jonathan may not have written a syllable during the period of his "dark years," but he did (if I may echo Regina) read and read and read, doing so at night and weekends, in his room, going through authors, books, and topics enough to keep twenty pairs of eyes occupied and to work toward the filling of twenty minds. *Psychology.* So long as that word is taken as meaning *everything*, it fits Jonathan. Montaigne. Erasmus. Rabelais. Freud. Jung. Adler. Erikson. Horney. *The Phantom Tollbooth. Dune. Principia Mathematica.* Galileo.

•

The only child of intelligent, well-intended, and yet remarkably cold parents, Jonathan was exposed throughout his formative life to a kind of psychological absolutism. His parents clearly wanted to do well by their gifted son, just as they clearly wanted to do well *for* him. They did both of these things, but they did them with very little if any understanding of his interior life. Although both the mother and the father were intellectually gifted, they were also unusually timid emotionally. They lived in fear, although in fear, precisely, of *what*—this was not an easy, or perhaps even a possible, thing for them to say. Fear of the unknown, certainly. But in what shape or form this unknown danger might come, if it ever did, or with what degree of force on the one hand, or with what deviousness, near-invisibility, or subtlety on the other—these were things they couldn't say, didn't want to think or speak of, and certainly not things that they wanted to be asked about by other people.

And "other people" included their own son.

Neither of the parents was able to understand the fact that since they were themselves thinking and feeling human beings, they thus possessed both an interior and an exterior life, and that these were of equal importance, and that this possession of—along with a *consciousness of*—both an interior and an exterior life or sentience was the only thing that made it possible for one person to be aware of another person in any other than *a purely surface way*. They had no idea that only this possession of an inner and an outer self, along with *an awareness of each*, was the gift that provided human beings with the ability to feel *empathy*.

This missing consciousness is why, on Jonathan's triumphant homecoming from the seminar in Poughkeepsie, his father showed no enthusiasm, emotion, joy, happiness, or praise. The father was no more able to perceive the son's inner life and thereby respond to it than he was able to perceive his own inner life and thereby respond to *it*. The result? The result was that nothing took place between them.

This cold, this absence, this being left absolutely alone in the father's simple gesture of turning away—these are what caused Jonathan to quit writing for two whole decades, and, with a ferocity and effort all but unimaginable, still manage somehow to come out of those dark years alive.

3

Illness can sometimes have a symbolic dimension, a pitiful or even eerie appropriateness. This was the case with Jonathan's father. At the start of the 1990s, he began having barely noticeable symptoms of a dementia that developed slowly but was to continue manifesting itself through the decade, as if it were wrapping him in layer after layer of some extremely soft material that gradually and painlessly (so far as anyone could tell) insulated him from the world around him. Things from the very recent past were the first to leave him—what he had had for lunch, for example, where he had left his keys. These were followed by things from the middle past—places, names, dates from his working life. Unrelentingly, the past grew closer and closer and closer to the present, until in time there remained no distance at all between them. His own parents ceased to be, his two siblings, his wife, and then disappeared also his son Jonathan.

When his father died (in 1999), Jonathan was still in his old childhood room, but he was very soon to leave it. By then, he had met Regina, or, more accurately, had re-met her, since the two of them had grown up on the same street in Queens and up through eighth grade had gone to the same schools. Regina was the person who brought Jonathan out from his black decades. She brought him out of his old room, she brought him out of Wall Street, and she brought him out of the Queens neighborhood that—up until then—they'd both thought of as home.

Regina graduated from Queens College in 1978 and afterward enrolled in a four-year program at New York University leading to a master's in social work. After getting the MSW, she worked in the field for three years, up to 1985, a time when Jonathan was still in the midst of his dark era. In that year, notably, Regina joined forces with an NYU classmate, and together they organized, developed, and instituted a business of their own, a program of counseling, placement, and care for the needy, especially those who were in advanced age or even facing death.

She proved adept at the work, as did her business partner, although of the two Regina clearly seemed the more suited to it temperamentally. As time went on, in any case, the pair took on additional help, both consulting and clerical, and eventually they moved the practice into an office space near St. Joseph's Hospital. The business prospered and the years passed while Regina continued living in Queens—where, one Saturday in 1996 on their old street in Fresh Meadows, she bumped into Jonathan and stood there with him for more than twenty minutes catching up. This was eighteen years after college, sixteen years after the beginning of Jonathan's dark period, and three years before his father's death. There was about to be great change. Months after the meeting on their old street, they would be living together not in Queens but in a co-op apartment on the upper west side of Manhattan; Jonathan would not only have left Wall Street but would be working half time as technical, clerical, and electronics support staff for Regina's practice; and he would be within another couple of years or so of beginning to write again.

·

I can't help noticing the balance as I thread my way through these events and changes in Jonathan's life. Symmetry. It throws me into a "no exit" kind of fear, even horror.

A person could argue that Jonathan's retreat into his dark years was inevitable after his realization that he had no father—no father, that is, who could hear him, listen to him, reciprocate feelings, respond to him. No father with empathy.

If Jonathan's father had been capable of empathy, he wouldn't have turned away from Jonathan, the way he did, in the kitchen, in Queens, that evening in the spring of 1980.

It will seem cruel and heartless for me to say it. But the dementia that settled in on Jonathan's father in a sense changed nothing. He was already, before the disease came, sealed up inside himself. The dementia simply made the seal perfect.

·

The next large turn in the drama is just as fearsome. When the absence of his father was made incontrovertibly clear to him, Jonathan wasn't able to invent any course of action other than withdrawal. The father had never engaged with the son. Then with his later dementia, followed by his death, he disappeared entirely.

•

Years later, after he had left Wall Street; after he had moved with Regina into Manhattan and had become a part of her practice; and then after he had begun writing again, around the end of the year 2000—the first thing he did was reach out and get back in touch with K. O. May.

•

He needed a father.

4

It was as though the end had been built in with a satanic perfection. A little bit like one of the ancient dramas. No escape would be allowed for anyone.

•

K. O. May was the same man he had been two decades ago, excepting for the diagnosis of Parkinson's disease gifted to him a year or two previously. But he recognized Jonathan, greeted him heartily, welcomed him warmly, made it quite clear that he was still fascinated by this brilliant ex-student who had—inexplicably—gone out of sight for twenty years. Why had this happened? What could have brought such a thing about?

Talk. Jonathan and his well-known mentor, now once again found, thrived on talk in the same way I was to experience talk in my own friendship with Jonathan a decade later. Conversation. Exploration. Looking deeply into everything.

In those days, May's disease hadn't yet taken any visible or noticeable toll on him—on his ability to reason, talk, read, even to write. He was at work on what, as it happened, would be his last book, an ambitious political-philosophic novel called nothing less than *The Republic*, a work he and Jonathan talked about frequently and at great length, discussing its direction and reading sections of it aloud as the book grew to completion (usually May would read aloud to Jonathan, although sometimes they traded roles, at such times as May wanted to listen more objectively, as it were, from a slightly greater distance). The book was published in 2017 (May died in early 2019), and when I read it a year later I found myself by turns stunned, mystified, and exhilarated, in much the same complexity of ways I'd felt reading the likes, say, of Thomas Mann, books like *The Magic Mountain* or *Doctor Faustus*.

In my heart I was fairly certain that *The Republic* served both as model and inspiration for Jonathan's own magnum opus, *The Institution*—a book, however, as I said earlier, I'm now all but certain I will never see, just as it's also likely I may never again see its author.

.

From the early months of 2001 on up to K. O. May's death, Jonathan made weekly visits to his mentor, almost without fail. At the start, these visits more or less picked up where the Poughkeepsie seminar had left off, except that now the conversation ranged much more widely than it had then and the pedagogic element was less highlighted. Even at this time, May was working on *The Republic*, sharing segments of it with Jonathan as the pages became ready, soliciting his quondam student's criticisms and responses. But years are short periods of time, especially when they are like hourglasses measuring out processes of loss, degeneration, and decay. The previously latent symptoms of May's illness gradually became visible, first in matters of coordination, then in tremors, balance, and mobility. The writer still insisted on going outdoors alone, until he once became inexplicably paralyzed halfway across

Amsterdam Avenue near 106th Street and found himself pelted helplessly by horns, curses, and the squeal of tires. After that incident, Mary Beth hired a home-care nurse to stay with him on weekdays for the eight hours that she herself was at work. Even after his ability to speak became compromised, May pushed ahead with *The Republic*, and after that time Jonathan's role changed, at least in part, since he was now the one who was asked to read aloud the new pages of the book, alert to May's signals—a nod meaning continue, a raised finger meaning pause—of approval or disapproval. He was still able to use his keyboard up to the end, when the manuscript, in its two large boxes, was at last sent off to be converted into galleys.

•

Around this time, on an autumn afternoon in 2011, I met Jonathan when he looked down at me and asked, "Are you an academic, by any chance?"

5

The loss of two fathers in a row, incalculably different from one another in most ways but alike in how they were removed from life: Reduced incrementally to near silence; then into absolute silence; then winked out like candles snuffed or stars collapsed in on themselves.

•

I can't help but feel that from this point on—for "this point" let me take 2017, when *The Republic* came out—can't help but feel that from this point on there occurs a change in time itself. Time speeds up. It begins going so fast that a person can't—*can't*—keep up with it.

Along with this acceleration, other things—terrible things—

began happening. Still, before this "dreadful acceleration" began picking up speed like a runaway train, there'd been some years, I admit, that still rambled by slowly enough to allow for contemplation, thought, pensiveness, even for *achievement*, if I may be allowed to put it that way. I mentioned before that in 2013 I brought out Jonathan's second volume of poems and in 2016 his hilarious short novel, *Pulling the Plug*. Even I was still able to work, think, ponder, sometimes even to *write*. In that same year, 2013, now so comfortably distant and quaint-sounding, I published a novel, albeit with the less-than-affirming title of *The Decline and Fall of the American Nation*. On the dedication page appeared the words *For What Was*.

Then the collapse. My own wife, Zoë, was diagnosed in the summer of 2018 with small cell lung cancer and died a year later, just months before the tidal wave of genocide, lies, deceit, corruption, madness, and hypocrisy was made visible to us all and set me on the blood-drenched path of trying to write *Doom in Slow Motion: A Writer's Notebook from the Years of the Great Covid-19 Terrorism and Genocide Campaign*.

Correction: The vast flood of genocide, deceit, corruption, and murder was made visible not "to us all" but to "*some* of us."

In that tiny alteration of phrasing, after all, lies the poisonous kernel of the dread and ruinous story I'm telling.

•

Then Regina herself went strange, seemed miserable, got edgy, pulled at her chain—the chain that Jonathan, before then, hadn't even known existed. Neither of Regina's parents were still living, and her sole close relative, a slightly older and very mean, selfish, and thoughtless sister, had died in the late autumn of 2019. This was the period when I heard her say to Jonathan in a voice well larded with sarcasm, "With you, everything is just psychology, psychology, psychology all the time, isn't it," and I couldn't help but wonder what kind of fears had been raised in Regina by her sister's death.

In any case, change was everywhere. Living together no longer seemed workable to either of them, and Jonathan spent a number of weeks following up leads and looking at apartments that were both nearby and also suitable for Regina. Her health—*and* her mobility—had weakened markedly in recent years, and finding an apartment that was right for her took some time. Then, once she was moved and settled, the question arose of a new place for Jonathan himself to move to in a cutting of expenses that was made necessary under the new arrangements. He found a studio apartment two blocks away, on a low floor, tiny, in the back of the building, but large enough—barely—to hold all of his books. Once he was moved in, his books lined the entirety of every wall, floor to ceiling, with openings only for doors and windows, so that he outdid Proust in needing no cork for the walls, or Dr. Faustus, living at peace in the very midst of his greatest treasures.

.

I propose that we leave him there, in that room, alone. I propose that we leave him there for however long may be necessary.

Poor Jonathan, damned.

6

The most shocking of the "news" began arriving halfway or so through March, just as the weather was sprinkled with the first harbingers and brushstrokes of spring.

Almost every bit of what we were told, of course, was lies. Ninety-five percent lies, the rest malevolently skilled distortion.

From the start, even in the planning, it was the Goebbels tactic, the telling of a lie so big people couldn't help but believe it. So big they couldn't *not* believe it. It was—it is—a program of terrorism. Fill people with wonder, awe, fear. Once they're terrified, they'll do anything you want them to.

All lies all the time.

All the lies fit to print.

You couldn't breathe the air without breathing in the lies.

•

I understand perfectly well that my subject here is Jonathan Fried. Or that Jonathan Fried is *supposed* to be my subject.

The terrible thing, however, is that now, here, at this point, it seems to me as though there's nothing further to be said, or to be shown, or chronicled, about him.

Like all of us, Jonathan evolved out of an enormous, long, deep past. He emerged from that past when he was born into *another* past, this one made up of a mixture of the present and the past, his own present and his parents' past. He struggled, then was pulled forcibly back. He struggled again, and again was pulled forcibly back. Then things fell apart. And then he— the striving, devoted, brilliant, sensitive, achieving Jonathan— went blind.

He wouldn't—couldn't?—see the truth. Instead, he saw the lies, he heard the lies, and, for reasons absolutely unknown to me, rather than seeing through them, he took them as true.

•

Something was dreadfully missing. Something was *tragically* missing.

People by the dozens—make that hundreds, thousands, millions—couldn't believe what they were hearing, so *absolutely frightening* these things were: And therefore they *did* believe these false and unseen things.

And then, very soon after, they really did see, with their

own eyes, other things that indisputably and by empirical observation *were in fact* happening—lockdowns, closings, maskings, one-way-street arrows on supermarket floors, six-feet-of-separation rules enforced assiduously—and they took these secondary and resultant things as proof that the *first* things must have been (and must now remain) even more true than they'd been (wrongly) taken as being the *first* time around.

The lies fed to the nation and world almost immediately led to the creation of a kind of self-reinforcing feedback loop. Sixty years ago, back in college, in freshman English, I remember learning about fallacies in logic. One of my favorites was *post hoc ergo propter hoc*, or "after this therefore because of this," exemplified by the false assumption that a person's having forgotten his or her umbrella when leaving the house in the morning is what made rain fall in the afternoon.

Of *course* the lockdowns were no proof (and had no proof) that there were germs everywhere that would kill us all if we didn't separate ourselves from one another, put on masks, and cower inside our houses.

But they came nevertheless, the lockdowns. With no good reason behind them that had to do with logic, medical evidence, historical precedent, or common sense, the lockdowns were imposed nevertheless. They became law. They destroyed multitudes, sickened thousands, brought to nations widespread penury, ugliness, hopelessness, despair.

•

God knows, it was no fun. Things fell into a kind of unreality and stasis. Even the everyday sounds of the city seemed either absent or oddly muted—except for the sirens, they being louder than ever, painfully so. But everything else was curiously diminished. Traffic up and down Broadway, for example, was half or a third of its usual volume, often less. For pedestrians, crossing against the light was easy, since often there wasn't a car, bus, or truck to be seen for three or even four blocks up or down the avenue. The city felt lonely in a way it hadn't felt before in all of my fifty years living here.

The essential thing, I reasoned, was to go on living, as much as possible, as though a vast but invisible net of madness and insanity had *not* been thrown over the nation, or the world. Other people, countless other people, *were* now mad by merit of their having swallowed, and their continuing to swallow, the lies and false terrors spread and paraded everywhere around them, terrors that were more and more frequently intensified by repetition, by onerous and oppressive rulings (no more than three inside a store at a time), by closings of churches, schools, libraries, theaters, meeting halls, and not least by the hysterical and unrelenting reports, day after day, false or not, of ever-rising tallies of the dead.

The end of March was balmy and bright, with April following after, sweet and sunny. The contrast between so lovely a spring and so ugly, deceived, and crippled a population was both awful and inescapable. I was lonely, yes—going on a year, at that time, without Zoë—but I was determined to live in as normal a way as possible. I spent a great deal of time at my keyboard, working fruitlessly on *Doom in Slow Motion*, and an equally great deal of time reading. This I did in the living room, in my spot at one end of the sofa, leaning into the corner there just as I'd done for all the years Zoë and I had spent our evenings in that room, reading. Each day that was fine, and many were, I made a point of walking out in the later part of the afternoon, usually down 99th Street and across Riverside Drive into the park, then down the park's winding paths to the river itself, where I would commune for a certain length of time, breathing the air—sometimes ocean-scented, sometimes freshwater—deep into my lungs.

If I had set out later than usual, or if I had communed at the river's edge for a longer time than normal, I would still be making my way home at the time of the seven o'clock cacophony instead of being once again in my living room, on the couch, reading.

Of the many symbols of the depravity and ruin being rained down upon an ignorant humanity, the "cacophony," as I called it (though only to myself), seemed to me possibly the most revealingly pathetic and blind. At exactly seven o'clock, the quietest moment of these early-summer evenings, windows would open and from inside emerge the beating of pots and pans, the unleashing of whistles, the shrilling of noise-makers, and the shouting of voices, while up and down the avenues and side-streets car horns would honk and blare in a toneless, tattered, underlying stratum of sound.

This aural pageantry troubled me greatly and lowered my spirits deeply. I knew that it was raised each evening as a way of honoring and giving thanks to hospital and health-care workers, but I also knew, from all of my reading and study, that the health-and-hospital industry represented one of the most menacingly destructive—and guilty—elements at work in the entire and murderous "emergency." I remember those days so clearly, the long days running through June, July, and August of 2020, and the evenings as well, not always happily by any means—*any* means—but vividly indeed. Most often I would be back from my walk to the river by the time the cacophony took place, and in fact most often I would have poured a glass of pinot noir and would be back in my living room, at my place on the couch, reading. In the very first days of the cacophony I would get up from the couch when it began, go to the open window, and lean out to see what I could see. Usually not much. Hundreds and hundreds of windows to be seen—across the street, up the street, down the street—but in only one or two, maybe two or three, would I see anyone else, and even then not necessarily anyone making noise, but people simply, like me, peering out to see the nothing that was there to be seen.

And yet the noise was very real, very loud, and very commanding. The acoustics of the city's streets, facades, walls, buildings, alleyways—these are tricky, intricate, and unpredictable. One time, having lingered down at the river's edge longer than usual, I found myself on the corner of West End and 99th Street waiting for the light as the cacophony began—and although I could see only very few people leaning out of windows and calling or clapping or banging or blowing, the sounds swirling around me were voluminous, dense, swirling, and loud, as though thousands and thousands of people were creating them.

Almost always, however, as I said, I was at home reading when it began. After the first few times, I no longer got up from the couch, no longer went to the window, no longer looked out. My habit instead was to pause in my reading and stay right where I was, as patient as I could make myself, and *wait*. I would listen, hear the familiar cowbell, the familiar wooden spoon beating on a soup pot, the familiar shouts, shrieks, cries, sirens, and horns—and wait until at last they began to die away, one sound going silent after another, until a final shout, a last bang of spoon on metal pot, would end the event and let the evening once again seep calmly into the streets.

This, in the spirit of accuracy, was what took place in the summer of 2020, close to a year before I broke with Jonathan Fried, and therefore also close to a year before things fell apart and time sped up. But in some ways I have come to think of these periods and events as having blended together, almost as if some of them were happening at the same time as others, whether such a thing might be possible or not.

But I think of myself in my living room, reading, then putting my book down and gazing into space as I wait for the relief I know I will feel when the cacophony comes to its end.

And Jonathan? I think of Jonathan at that same moment, two blocks away, in his room on a low floor, at the back of the building, in a chair, at a table, gazing at one of his book-lined walls.

What does he hear? What does he think? What does he do?

I have no choice but to let him be.

Jonathan. Poor Jonathan. Jonathan, damned.

7

Later (much later: It's now three days before Christmas 2022) I think of the things that have happened as if they were parts of a board game. By this time, every piece has either been eliminated from the board or forced into a weakened position. Jonathan's father, of course, has been absent for a long time, as also, now, has that piece's symbolic replacement, the writer K. O. May. Regina has been moved off to one side, where she lacks any other pieces to give her protection. I myself am no longer in the game, and so I am also missing. As for Jonathan, he has (why? for protection? or?) gone through something like a castling. He has retreated into a corner of the board, protected there by his fortress of books, a place where, at the same time, he has also forfeited the ability to move with any kind of nimbleness—or perhaps the ability to move at all. That would make it endgame.

I parted with Jonathan in June 2021, eighteen months ago now. A few weeks after that, in late July, I called him on the telephone and talked for a long time; and in early November I wrote a letter—an "open" letter meant to be a chapter in *Doom in Slow Motion*, though I also sent it to Jonathan as a piece of personal correspondence.

After that, silence.

I moved on. The world slipped into greater murderousness than ever under the genocidal diktat of its medical tyranny. And Jonathan, so far as I knew, did nothing to defend himself, protect himself, or cure himself.

Then, early last month, when I finally did learn what he was doing, I was shocked enough that I set out at once to write the words you are now reading. And to give them the dread title that I did.

.

I met Barbara Powell probably eight or nine years ago at the Regional bar, back when my wife Zoë and I were near-regulars there, and then afterward true regulars. Around that same time we had also gotten to know Tony Stonefield through the music he and his band played Sunday afternoons a few blocks uptown at the now-gone Picnic Café. It turned out that Tony and Barbara themselves were already well acquainted, since for a number of years Tony had sung as baritone in Barbara's vocal quartet. After a run of slightly more than a decade, that quartet—in 2014—disbanded. Tony went on with his band—and, more seriously, with his writing—while Barbara continued in her old position as professor of voice and director of choral music at Hunter College. She retired from that post in 2020. And on the sixth of November two years later came her seventieth birthday.

After Zoë's death, in July of 2019, I gradually came to be more closely acquainted with Barbara—especially since both of us continued to frequent Regional—until, by the time her seventieth birthday came around, we had grown into an intimate pair who, among many other things, set about throwing a birthday party.

Barbara had a great many friends, some dating from her arrival in New York, now forty years ago, others from among the many friends she acquired during her quartet's performance and touring years, still others from Hunter College, and of course a good number simply from the neighborhood we shared, and, needless to say, from the Regional bar.

And I must now mention that she also knew Jonathan Fried, to whom, a good ways back, she'd been introduced by me. Nor was she about to forget him when it came time to send out party invitations.

Barbara, allow me to say, is not only a human being extraordinarily gifted in her talents as artist and musician, but she is notable and rare also in being more abundantly possessed than anyone else I've known in the laudable traits of fidelity, generosity, and compassion.

It's no wonder that Barbara has many friends. It's no wonder, either, that my break with Jonathan was something that troubled her considerably. And it's no wonder that she now wanted to reach out to him, invite him to the party, maybe even bring him and me back together.

·

If what follows is to make any sense, it behooves me to explain myself at least to a certain degree. And so. By the time of Barbara's party, I hadn't changed in any significant way from what I'd been at the time of my break from Jonathan. It was still apparent to me that the world was in the midst of a war both unscrupulous and lethal; that everything human was under vicious attack by inhuman ideologues and zealots; that the attack was massive, deadly, all-important, and insidious; and that only the waking up of a sleeping, narcotized population to the truth of what was being done to them—only this popular awakening could spark the awareness necessary for the creation of a resistance capable of leading to organized revolt against the secretive, determined, genocidal murderers busily at work toward the elimination of us all.

I broke with Jonathan because of his refusal—or his inability, even worse—to acknowledge the truth of any of these atrocities, or of the thousands of lies being broadcast in support of them, or even of the extraordinary danger he had put himself in by following the "recommended" course of repeated injections of the "vaccine."

He and I, Jonathan had argued again and again, could go on just as we had in the earlier years of our friendship. Nothing had changed, really, he insisted. We could still talk about literature, art, and aesthetics, about our own books and our own ideas about writing. We could still talk about Jonathan's monumental effort in writing *The Institution*, and about the progress he was making with it....

But, no, I couldn't do it. Perhaps in that one particular way I *had* changed in the months leading up to our break and in the time since. No, I wouldn't—*couldn't*—go on as if "nothing had changed." Imagine an ocean liner steaming across the Pacific Ocean on a pleasure voyage between, say, Los Angeles and Melbourne. Imagine yourself as the single person in the world who *knows* that this liner is destined to sink as it crosses the Mariana Trench, disappearing forever along with every living being it carried. Would you—the person who *knew*—accept an invitation to lead a literary discussion group during the crossing, or to lead an on-board Elderhostel in its discussions of the history of western philosophy, or...

Friendship universally has about it great numbers of delicacies and subtleties, but given the world as it is now, the vast majority of friendships must depend either on the shared ignorance of those who are friends or, in a case like mine and Jonathan's, upon the superhuman ability of one party to suppress a certain truth, hiding it from the other, even though the possessor of that truth sees it as being a thing of an absolute, utmost, adamantine urgency.

The friendship among me, Barbara Powell, and Tony Stonefield came about partly because of shared interests but also partly because of shared *views*, these being views about the "medical emergency." For a considerable period of time—beginning well before my break with Jonathan—we fell into the habit of getting together on Sundays at five to talk about books on the one hand and our own writing on the other. We gathered—and still do—at one of the tables in the back of Regional, whose opening time of five o'clock determined the opening time of our "class."

I mention these things because of my effort to describe Jonathan—my effort, I mean, to describe the breadth, the sheer immensity and depth, of the breach, the *gulf*, between us. In our "class," we used to set writing assignments for ourselves, due the following week, and one that often got repeated was an assignment to create a narrative in two hundred words or fewer that didn't lose sense but, instead, maintained *some* kind of significant meaning through narrative.

We came up with interesting things. Here's one of my own that satisfied me fairly well but that would be anathema, less than silence, to Jonathan:

A Perfect Morning

Lies are truth. Sickness is health. Fraud is candor.

Madness is sanity.

Such words and phrases were going through his head as he took the elevator down, passed through the foyer, then went out the front entrance of his building onto the street.

The morning was beautiful. The sky was clear and actually blue for once, not covered by the usual steel-gray haze, as if skim milk had been poured into it. The air was fresh, pleasantly cool against his skin.

He walked down to the corner, where greetings came from the Yemini guys sitting outside their housewares store. The same came from Manuel at the flower stand. Manuel's cat, when he bent down to scratch her ears, rolled onto her back to welcome a belly rub.

He walked to the end of the block and got a large coffee from Lenny's Bagel Shop. Then he went back the way he had come, carrying the coffee past the cat, past Manuel, and past the Yeminis at their store.

When he was in his apartment again, in the front room, at his desk, coffee near at hand, he opened his computer, drew its keypad toward him, and typed two sentences:

"Today is May 20th, 2021. Our 'leaders' want all of us dead as soon as possible."

•

As the time drew nearer for her party, Barbara sent out invitations, a goodly number of them, including one to Jonathan. She showed me his response:

Dear Barbara,

First, I wish you a very happy birthday! And thank you so much for inviting me.

I am concerned that Malcolm might not welcome my presence, and in fact might be quite angry to see me there, which is not a particularly good thing at a birthday celebration. As you no doubt know, last year, to my dismay and amazement, Malcolm ended our friendship because I did not (and do not) agree with his view that Covid is a hoax and the vaccine is part of a massive conspiracy, of which Bill Gates is a part, to kill six billion people and implant chips in us all.

If Malcolm's view of me has changed back to that which characterized the years of our friendship, I would of course be delighted to attend. The loss of my connection with Malcolm as such a valued part of my life was for me a source of sadness.

Please let me know your thoughts, Barbara.

In any case, again, I wish you a very happy birthday!

xo Jonathan

•

I said earlier that I hadn't changed in any significant way since my break with Jonathan. I stick with that claim and only hope I may be excused for mentioning it again.

Jonathan is the one who has changed. In a most, most dreadful way.

How this can be, I'm unable to fathom. I can't begin to understand it. Hard enough is simply trying to believe it.

•

When she asked me about it, I assured Barbara that, no, I would in no way be "angry" to see Jonathan at the party. In fact, I went on, it seemed to me a childish notion to think such a thing.

·

I realized that Jonathan hadn't understood at all. All this time, from the start of 2020 on through nearly the end of 2022, he'd thought I was "angry" at him. No. Not in the least. Being in the company of Jonathan didn't make me angry. It was something quite different—and much worse. Being with Jonathan had become intolerable. Being with Jonathan had become *unbearable*.

·

I don't mean personally, if such a word can possibly do justice to what I mean. No, there was nothing personal in this awful feeling that arose in me. Jonathan Fried was outwardly the same man now as he had been when I first met him, eleven years back, when he said to me in his friendly, wry, slightly bemused way, "Are you an academic, by any chance?"

He was still one of the smartest people I'd ever known. He was still the same as before—wry, amusing, quick-witted, perceptive, observant, invariably well-spoken.

It's just that now, along with all of that, he had also gone mad.

Barbara's party was big, with close to sixty people on the guest list, and I offered up my own apartment for the occasion, since its five-and-a-half rooms offered much more space than Barbara's own two-and-a-half. The party was a great success, with people eating, talking, drinking, catching up with one another and also of course with Barbara. And there was music as well, of a kind that made me think of James Joyce's *The Dead*, when at four or five different moments one of the quondam members of Barbara's quartet would hush the crowd by offering up a song or aria, with even Tony Stonefield at one point, standing in the foyer where we'd positioned the pianist, offering up Mozart's *Deh, Vieni Alla Finestra.*

Jonathan—the only one that night wearing a mask—arrived after the party was well underway and stayed only half an hour or so. I happened to be in the front room when he came in. That room was crowded enough that I couldn't easily move, but the apartment is arranged in such a way as to give a clear view through the foyer to the front door, so I could see him come in. I gave him a wave, but I'm sure he didn't see it, since he went directly into the dining room where, I knew, Barbara was helping lay out the buffet.

When the crowd thinned slightly in the front room, I made my way through the foyer and into the dining room, where I spotted Jonathan and Barbara standing together in a far corner. I made my way over to them and made greetings to Jonathan, whereupon Barbara touched his arm, and then mine, made her excuses, went across the room and disappeared into the kitchen.

And so there we were. Jonathan. Me. Greetings. Customary amenities, the passing back and forth of. And then, after a moment or two, I told him that I had one immense question and that it was a question of extreme importance.

I asked him how work was progressing on *The Institute.*

8

"Oh," he said. "That. You know, with all these health concerns. I haven't looked at it."

He turned away as another party guest touched his elbow and greeted him. But I had understood well enough. *The Institute* was gone. For all its merit, complexity, and importance, Jonathan had dropped it in something like the way a boy might drop the string leading to his toy sailboat on the pond in Central Park.

After all, Jonathan had listened to the falsehoods and taken them as true. He had heard the aural pageantry, had heard the cacophony, and, drinking it in as if it were truth, had closed his eyes and raised his face to let it wash over him. All evening, for the rest of Barbara's party, I thought about him. I even said goodbye to him and, having withdrawn again to my vantage point in the living room, watched as he let himself out the front door, his mask leading, the hem of his long raincoat following.

It seemed to me that something must have shrunk, withered, and collapsed inside Jonathan. It seemed to me that the best qualities in him must have crumbled, dissolved, or been eaten away as if by the work of some invisible but virulently corrosive agent. Jonathan Fried, one of the smartest people I ever knew, had chosen lies over truth. He had chosen death over life. He had chosen to use the medical emergency, built on lies, as his own private weapon in his own version of Russian roulette.

9

I think of Jonathan as a man driven mad by three fathers.

His own father was the first, the father who abandoned his son. Then came K. O. May, who did the same thing, although this abandonment came about not through his own will but through the tyranny of disease. And the third?

It may be impossible to name the third. But this third father is a monster of unbounded cruelty and power. This "third father" is the same liar and deceiver that brought into existence the dreadful ritual of seven-o'clock noise-making that I called aural pageantry: The outward expressing of an inner emptiness, weakness, suggestibility, pliability, ignorance, naiveté.

This third father is the greatest liar on earth.

This third father is the most evil thing in existence.

Treading over the ruins left behind by the first two fathers, this third father strangles, threatens, and starves in ways that make him able to reduce even a genius like Jonathan Fried to a passive wreck who can't believe his own eyes, can't believe his own ears, can't trust in his own powers of logic or reason.

Horrible to think, worse to say, but Jonathan at Barbara's party was like K. O. May when he walked onto Amsterdam Avenue near 106th Street and, halfway across, found himself paralyzed, able to do nothing but stand there helplessly, pelted by horns, curses, and the squeal of tires.

The "vaccine," the thing the third father says people must receive if they aren't to fall sick and die, has so far killed 3,591,100 people in just one country, the country that happens to be our own. And the number of those not killed but merely paralyzed, incapacitated, made unfit for employment, or otherwise injured: 62,602,800.

Such is the aural pageantry, such is the cacophony, that can ruin and beguile even those who are geniuses.

Jonathan Fried, old friend, god bless you.

Jonathan Fried. Poor Jonathan. Jonathan, damned.

7

1

Minutiae

More or less the same as any other day, he was at his desk, gazing out the window. He was thinking about time. He was thinking about the half-century that had somehow slipped by, as if by a cruel kind of magic, and about the changes that had come about during it.

He had lived in the same apartment—this one, with this front window and this view of the street—for fifty-two years. He moved in on August 1st, 1971, and today was July 13, 2023. It was a few minutes past one in the afternoon.

In all his time living here, he had never seen fewer people passing by on the street below—at this particular time of day—than he did now.

.

He felt it more every day, as he had for the past two years—no, longer than two years now: The disorienting sense that catastrophic, shameless crimes were taking place around the world and yet that no one was noticing—or doing anything about them.

On the other hand, as he told himself over and over, this feeling must be nothing new. People throughout history must have had this same sense of disbelief and unreality. In antiquity, when their city fell to the Spartans, the Athenians must have felt the same all-consuming disbelief and fear. Or the French, when Hitler entered Paris. Or the Cherokee on the Trail of Tears. The sheer immensity of the atrocities brought down upon them, upon their families, people, nation. Their world upside down.

History. He revered history and read a good deal of it, but he had never especially cared for its practitioners. Why was it—as he had noticed for most of his life, decade after decade— that historians themselves were so often *cold*? All the way back as an undergraduate at New College, over sixty years ago, there had been Charles Cummings, certainly no longer among the living—he'd be nearly a hundred and fifty if he were still alive—but back then Cummings was the living emblem of the arch, chill, fastidiously condescending, humorless practitioner of *history*. He had been a bloodless figure more akin to, say, Arthur Dimmesdale (so it seemed then to the eighteen-year-old and poorly read Malcolm Reiner) than to anyone with warmth in his veins, passion in his heart, or love of humankind.

What was it about them, historians, that made them so seldom ever to want *change*, or to work for it, certainly not change for the better? Matt Tubridy, at the dreadful Actaeon College, was a good example. Or that fellow named David, the one at the bar in Regional whom Malcolm called—inaccurately—a bigot. David McCall. He was an ignoramus and a blowhard, but he hadn't shown *quite* enough deficiency of character to justify Malcolm's calling him a bigot. Close to it, but not quite. In any case, Malcolm did call him one. And McCall was, yes, a historian, an economic historian, one who wrote for major magazines and traveled through Asia and the Far East scraping up material for his articles and books. And yet even so, no matter what kind of criminality or oppression or cheating or injustice he came upon—instead of doing anything about them, he'd rather brag about knowing such things the way others might brag about the biggest fish they'd caught. The fact was that McCall didn't have a *moral* molecule in his body—that oversize and muscular body that put a major strain on the bar stool, that made him look like a fullback for the Covid Cannibals, *and* that for five minutes terrified Malcolm, all five-foot nine inches of him, into a fight-or-flight paralysis caused by the fear that one of Forbes' bowling-pin forearms was about to lift suddenly from the bar and smash a hairy fist right into his own face.

·

Absurd, he thought. It's even possible that he said the word out loud, or at least whispered it.

Behind him, the rooms of the apartment were silent. Nothing stirred. He continued gazing out the window even though he knew he should turn back to his keyboard and get on with his work.

On the street below, a person was walking from West End Avenue toward Broadway, and two people—although they weren't together—were making their way from Broadway toward West End.

On the other side of 99th Street rose the glass-paneled high-rise, all thirty-two floors of it, that had been built ten or so years before. The building's main entrance was on 99th Street, and as Malcolm sat at his desk looking out, one of the doormen, in his blue uniform, came out through a front door and, after looking each way, ambled over to the curb and stood with his toes extending just over its edge. He looked each way again. Checked his wristwatch. Then, before he turned and went back into the high-rise, he bent his head forward and, lazily, sent a ball of spit into the gutter.

It used to be so different, years ago, when Zoë was still living and the children were young. The neighborhood was filled with people then, and even on the plainest of days there would be the savor of a festive atmosphere. On weekend afternoons the family often went out together to one place or another, perhaps down to a playground in Riverside Park or—when the children were older—on expeditions for clothing, followed afterward, often, by a walk uptown two or three blocks to Sal and Carmine's for pizza or calzone, or other times downtown for ice cream and café au lait at the Rica bakery. They would sit at the long S-shaped counter, considering themselves lucky to have found four stools together. Malcolm remembered vividly what it was like on those Saturday or Sunday afternoons, the pleasant feeling of adventure that came simply from leaving the apartment and going out the front door of the building onto 99th St., then turning right and going the half block down to the intersection with Broadway. Broadway runs slightly downhill on its way south from 99th St. to 96th St., then climbs uphill again as it continues the three or four blocks to 94th St. and 93rd St. On those weekend afternoons, if Malcolm stood where 99th St. meets Broadway and looked south, he could see the sidewalk all the way down to 93rd and it would look like a slowly moving river, a conveyor belt filled edge to edge with people, all blended together into a solid stream.

Now, though, it wasn't that way at all. The crowds on the sidewalks were sparse and thin no matter what day of the week or time of day. Some time back, Malcolm gave up making coffee in the apartment, and now, when he went out mid-morning each day to get his coffee from the bagel shop uptown two blocks, there were so few cars and trucks that he was able half the time to cross Broadway without waiting for the green light—the avenue often stretching all the way down to 96th and up to 102nd without there being visible a single car or truck.

•

It's upside down, Malcolm thought. *It's inside out.* But then he corrected himself. The truth lay in neither of the things he had just said—or neither of the things he had just *thought*, since he wasn't sure whether he had said them aloud, or had said them in a whisper, or had said them at all.

Either way, he had been wrong. Or inexact.

The truth was something different. The truth was that the omnipresent criminality and the murderous satanism that had been allowed to grow up around the world had to do not with inside and outside, not with upside and down, but with things small and large, with the relationship between them. *That's it*, he thought. *That's* the problem. *That's* why people are allowing themselves to be destroyed. *That's* why whole populations have been rendered ignorant and mute. *That's* why entire masses become blind to their murderers and tormentors; *that's* why they don't believe in, don't so much as *look at*, the monsters who are raining the atrocities down upon them, let alone *see* the evil-doers or so much as *imagine* the horror....

Life has got to be made out of small things first, Malcolm thought, and large things second. *Yes.*

He turned away from the window and toward his desk, drew his keyboard closer, and began typing:

Isn't it true that in a sane and normal world, a world capable of being and remaining humane, that in such a world life must be comprised of small things first, and of large things only second?

And isn't it true that in that sane and normal world, if it's a world capable of being imbued and guided by the humane, these small things are the ones—the only ones—that can, must, and will serve to make the large things happen, and that this is how life inside a humanely balanced world has to be and ought to be?

Is there, in short, any other way for life to be organized if any human goodness is going to be able to survive and go on living inside of it?

Take the oak tree. It drops two thousand acorns, probably many more, and if the tree is lucky three or four of them will sprout, and of those perhaps one will take root. But one is a great many. The acorn is small but the oak tree is large. Immense. Thick, high, dense with foliage, a blessed shelter from the sun on a hot August afternoon when someone sits under it, leaning against its trunk.

Acorn. Then oak.

So it must be with our world if tyranny and mass murder are to end.

•

And then Malcolm said to himself: *I think I may be going insane.*

•

He fell asleep at his desk, head fallen forward, cradled in his forearms. He dreamt of something that had taken place almost seven decades before, when he was twelve years old. His best friend at that time was a kid named Charlie Scott, who lived on a farm half a mile down the road. A year younger than Malcolm, Charlie was nevertheless more curious, adventurous, and daring than Malcolm. The two friends roamed far and wide on the land that made up the farms they lived on. Once, at the most distant back property-line of Charlie's farm, they came upon an opening in an area that was otherwise wooded. It appeared that there had once been a house there, and a barn, although the grass had grown up to obscure most of what remained of their foundations. The boys pulled the grass aside and began to dismantle a number of the cinderblocks that were still intact. When Charlie pushed one block off the top of another, a hollow space was revealed in what had been the bottom of two cinderblocks, and in that space was now exposed a family of baby field mice. There were nine or ten of them, each smaller than a sewing thimble. They were hairless and blind, frantically climbing up onto one another, trying to find protection.

Malcolm, asleep, age eighty-one, head bowed and resting on his forearms, dreamed about those mice from seventy years before.

The date was Thursday, July 13, 2023, the time a few minutes past four in the afternoon.

2

Silence

1

I've given up talking. That is, I've given up speaking words aloud in order to convey anything more important than "half-pound of Swiss, please," for example, or "pumpernickel with chopped herring."

My reasons are immensely important, and also difficult to explain, or at least most of them are. I obviously can't explain them aloud, since I've given up talking. Writing them down, however, might be all right. What you're reading here, then, are words without words. Words without sound. Invisible words. Language invisible.

2

On a simple and personal level, it's a matter of my having grown tired of being taken for a madman. The Canadian wild-fires, for example. I have my thoughts about them, grounded in evidence. But no one will let me express these thoughts unless I pay for the privilege by "admitting" afterward that I'm crazy and that my notions are insane. I've got to agree, that is, in closing, to guffaw at myself along with the yukking others. If I don't accept these terms, I'll be ostracized, be left to drink alone. For a long time I wasn't ready for that kind of isolation. I went on betraying myself by avoiding conversation about anything I really wanted to talk about. This meant, however, that I was in effect—no, in actuality—relegating bar-talk to the same level of importance as ordering Swiss on rye or a bagel with butter.

It was a self-fulfilling prophecy. On those terms, an evening at the bar—so long as all the talk remained small—brought no more depth, meaning, or reward than saying thanks to somebody for holding the door. Maybe less.

In truth, it was worse than that. As my bar-mates went on with the small talk of their choice—movies, actors, television shows, maybe sports—I realized that in order to remain companionable, I had been required to commit suicide. I'd been required to smother the part of me that was most alert, observant, alive, the part in the greatest need of knowing the truth at any cost, the part that was most similar to the figure in the famous Munch painting, "The Scream."

My friends at the bar—Tom, Dave, Vicky, Carla, Roger, Helena—thought I was insane at those times when in fact I was being the most authentic, natural, and real. They preferred the lobotomized me, the one with his tongue cut out, the one gone blind. That's the one they liked.

3

"We're past the tipping point right now."

"... to make it sound like nature did it..."

"—so many facts that the so-called science community never mentions when they label everything with 'climate change' and try to frame it like it's some sort of a partly natural process. *There is nothing natural about the imploding planet that we're all passengers on, nothing natural about it."* [2]

4

Headline: "This factory breeds 30 million mosquitoes per week."[3]

5

Or vaccines. Let's talk about vaccines.

6

No, can't mention. Mustn't. And not just among my friends. The whole nation now deaf and blind.

The whole nation, in the millions upon millions. Blind. Deaf. Doomed.

Repeat after me:

Blind. Deaf. Doomed.

Until this point has come, the point we've now reached, the point where a person can't commingle, can't be one of the group, except—like in my case—by pretending not to *be* myself, pretending not to see what I see, read what I read, understand what I understand.

If I want to be sociable it's necessary first to be a liar, to lie like a rug. By both omission and commission. The requirement for admission to the club. I have to pretend nothing less than that I'm not myself—when I'm among those who, no matter what I do, secretly consider me insane.

So perfectly has the trap been set; so perfectly has the noose been tightened.

____

2 Geoengineering Watch Global Alert News, July 1, 2023, # 412 (Dane Wigington) - YouTube. Emphasis added.

3 This factory breeds 30 million mosquitoes per week. Here's why. | Bill Gates (gatesnotes.com)

7

It's like being caught inside a slowly closing circle of soldiers,
their bayonets leveled—aimed at me.
    Intolerable.
    But I know what I'll do.
    I'll stop going to the bar.
    I'll begin drinking alone, in my room.

3

The Death of Albert Einstein

Althea Clarke thought of the eighth grade as being of unusual and extreme significance for her students. This pivotal year— *her* year—had an almost immeasurable importance, she felt, since it was the last step in lower school and the final opportunity for students to prepare for their imminent graduation into high school.

Near the top of her aims was the development in her students of a strong and healthy taste for reading. She felt that the formation of such an appetite was not only of crucial importance in gaining a successful education, but that it remained a lifelong asset throughout adulthood.

In the furtherance of this aim, Miss Clarke was in the habit of escorting her students to the school library for a half period each week, usually on Fridays. After fifteen or twenty minutes with them, she would leave the room and hand over responsibility to the school librarian. Her aim in doing this was, first, to give the students an opportunity to browse on their own.

But she had a second aim as well. She very much wished, of course, that each pupil would leave the library with at least one new book in hand. This was part of the test. At the same time, there was a test within that test, and this second test had to do—through patient observation—with another way of allowing Miss Clarke to measure each student's interest, aptitude, and ambition in reading. Some of her students, she knew perfectly well, would leave the library without any new book at all. This was a part of the nature of things, a part of life. Miss Clark was fond—as her faculty colleagues were fully aware—of the sentiment that you can lead horses to water though not make them drink.

In spite of her pedagogical severity and rigor, and the ambition she had for her students, Miss Clark, in person, was pleasant, soft-spoken, and kind, in certain ways even self-effacing and meek.

It so happened that her classroom possessed large blackboards on both its front and back walls. Miss Clark made use of the front blackboard for various daily purposes of one kind or another. The board on the back wall, however, she used for the permanent display of various kinds of announcements, records, and achievements.

She prepared one large section of the rear blackboard, for example, in the manner of a large piece of graph paper, with carefully-ruled horizontal lines intersected with vertical ones.

At the left of each horizontal line she printed the name of a student, thirty-two in all. And across the top of the chart, designating each vertical line, she placed the numbers one through thirty.

Miss Clark prepared this chart near the beginning of the school year, sometime before September had come to an end. And with preparation of the chart the eighth grade reading competition began. There were no requirements in the competition other than the single one that each student read as many books as he or she might choose, and on completion of each one—whenever this might be—write a book report of approximately five-hundred words and submit this report to Miss Clarke.

The remainder of the competition may have been its most spectacular part. Each report, after its submission, would be graded. This grade would then be cited on the blackboard graph, so that not only would the *number* of books a student had read be cited there (up to a total of thirty), but cited also, for all to see, would be the *grade* the student's report had received.

Each grade, from "A" to "F," was indicated by the image of a star chalked into place in the appropriate square on the blackboard graph.

And the grade-value of each star was indicated by the color of the chalk that had produced it. The highest in value was etched in gold, followed by the colors of its four declining brethren: silver, red, yellow, and white.

•

As it happened, one of Miss Clarke's students in this long-ago time went by the name of Malcolm Reiner. Malcolm's experience of eighth grade fell in the school year 1954–1955, now approximately seventy-three years ago.

Malcolm remembers four things from the time he spent in eighth grade English under the tutelage of Miss Clarke.

It's doubtless true that he remembers many more than just four things. But these stand out in the sense that he *remembers* remembering them.

He remembers that Miss Clarke, trim, tidy, and small in person, invariably wore skirt-and-jacket suits composed of tweeds in winter and of other fabrics in warmer weather, at which times Miss Clarke would now and then doff her jacket and continue teaching in a very white blouse or shirt.

A second thing he remembers is misspelling a word in one

of his book reports. The word appeared in the phrase "naval officer," which he had spelled "navel officer." Miss Clarke circled the misspelled word in red and wrote the correction in the margin.

The third thing he remembers had to do with the graph on the blackboard. Admittedly, this memory is composed of what might be considered a number of "mini-memories," among them the remorse he felt at seeing how few stars appeared on, say, Denny Gardner's line, and how those few appeared only in stars alternating between yellow and white. More saliently, however, he remembers being in an unspoken competition with certain classmates, above all with Peter Hess, whose father was a professor at Old College, who tended to be a bully, and whose line of all-gold stars on the blackboard graph lengthened neck and neck with his own—until, sometime in the last few weeks of the school year, the absolutely unheard of thing happened: One morning there appeared on Peter's line a *white star*. From that time on, Peter submitted no more book reports and received no more stars, allowing Malcolm, alone in the class, to complete an unbroken row of thirty gold marks.

The last thing Malcolm remembers is the death of Albert Einstein.

He remembers this death because Miss Clarke took time at the end of class one day to talk to her students about the importance of the great man's passing. Doctors, she told her students, were in the process of undertaking posthumous examinations of Einstein's brain, and, notably, they were discovering that the great scientist's brain was exceptional in the number, depth, and complexity of its convolutions, folds, wrinkles, and channels.

These features of the brain had come about, she explained, as a result of the lifelong and unbroken seriousness, concentration, and profundity of Einstein's thinking.

In conclusion Miss Clarke explained to her students—with

a firm and serious emphasis—that each of them, throughout life, should do everything they could to live in emulation of Albert Einstein.

4

"Up Is Down," Said One

Once you start seeing common things in an unusual way, or once you begin looking at them in a manner even slightly different from the customary, your sense of reason can abandon you like a suddenly frightened bird, leaving behind a hollow space that can fill up quickly with madness.

When I lived in Europe in 1968–1969 (my first sojourn there), I gathered up a number of Peter De Vries novels. I'm not sure how many I read, but I know that among them were *The Mackerel Plaza*, *The Tunnel of Love*, and *The Blood of the Lamb*. In one, I remember, a man in a boarding house flattered his landlady at breakfast by telling her how much he loved her brioches, while privately he was referring to her breasts, by which he was obsessed. Elsewhere, a man—maybe the same guy—on a crowded sidewalk found himself suddenly staggered by the thought that the people around him all had *insides* and that these perfectly normal-looking men and women were kept alive by their innards: The bellows in their chests that pushed gasses out and drew them in again, gasses that became absorbed into small rivers of blood streaming through miles of vessels that reached to the very tips of fingers and toes, blood that also flooded the brain, all of this system of deep red moved along by a single muscle-motor that pumped, and pumped, and pumped....

I've been reminded lately—in myself—of that second De Vries character. I haven't become obsessed by people's innards, but I *have* found it impossible to keep myself from noticing their *heads*; I mean, specifically, the *size* of their heads, how enormous they are in proportion to the rest of the animal. Once I began noticing this quality of the human shape—absurdly top-heavy—it became impossible for me to ignore that ungainly round object balanced up there at the top, smug and pompously self-impressed, as if being carried around decade after decade in the best seat in the house for nothing more than the privilege of sight-seeing were the most natural thing in the world.

And then there was the equally laughable fact of the *neck*, that pipe-and-conduit-filled structure of bone and muscle that tirelessly balances the enormous head day after day, seldom complaining and never letting its burden fall off.

A person who has a long and slender neck with a smallish head on the top is hardly less of a mystery—of disproportion, attenuation—than is a professional footballer with a head the size of a Mini Cooper's engine sitting on a neck thicker than a bollard.

In the case of someone whose "reality principle" is slipping away, visions of this kind also pertain—I mean, that person's visions are likely to be equally mysterious, weird, and disproportionate. When someone loses the practice of seeing the world through eyes that are content to see in obedience to habit, familiarity, and custom; when that person begins, instead, to look at things as if he or she were seeing them for the first time; then almost anything previously taken as familiar and normal can become alarming, or absurd—or insane.

Today's date, as I write these words, is July 3rd, 2021, which means that for just around eighteen months, from mid-March of last year up to now, I have been struggling to hold on to the "sense of reason" that I mentioned in the opening of this piece. The experience—I'll call it the experience of going mad, since that's pretty much the fact of it—is one I've had many times before in my relatively long life, but never has this sickness—the sickness of being absolutely clear sighted—gone on for so long or been so resistant as now. This ailment *of seeing things as they really are* simply won't let me go, but it hangs on with a powerful, stubborn, fierce refusal to allow me to fall back into the lovely and sleep-like habit of seeing things not as they really are, but of seeing them, instead, as habit, custom, and familiarity have long *said* they are...

I'm seriously beginning to lose hope that recovery will ever come; I fear that I may never be able to make my eyes lie to me once again and thus bring me comfort, rest, and calm instead of the shock, dread, and horror they unvaryingly bring me now.

A week or two ago I was descending from the high floor I live on in my building when the elevator came to a stop, the door opened, and four young people got in, two men and two women, none of whom I had seen before. They were talking animatedly as the door opened, and without a break they continued talking animatedly as they stepped in and the door closed behind them. Being a polite sort of person, I stepped into a rear corner of the car so as to allow them their fair share of room—a simple gesture that, however, had the unintended and devastating effect (for me) of making it only the more impossible for me to avoid *observing* them. And there they were, so close that I could have touched them had I wanted to, their oversized heads nodding and wobbling atop their bone, tube, and-blood stuffed necks. None paid the least attention to me, and they went on talking as if I weren't there at all. But I *was* there, I *did* exist, and, short of closing my eyes or blindfolding myself, there was no escape, in this tiny space of the descending elevator, from the outrageous necessity not only of continuing to *observe* them but also of continuing to *hear* them. Words, phrases, sentences were emitted helter-skelter from mouths; lips were shaped, moved, reshaped; laughter was sent out; heads tossed; mouths opened wide; tongues and teeth were displayed.

"Up is down," said one.

"Out is in," another.

"Oh, yes! I *believe it*," a third.

"Lies are truth!"

"I lived in the city for five years then went to Boston," said one.

"I'm *so* happy with myself! Aren't *you*?"

"Yes, and now *we're absolutely safe*."

"Isn't it wonderful?"

"Which did you have, one or two?"

"Life is death," said one, and the four voices united in a peal of laughter.

Once again, in the way it invariably happens to me lately, under the present tyranny, I understood with certainty that these talkers believed every word they were saying or had said; that each of them was being purely and absolutely candid; and that (being incapable of doing anything else) *they were talking about the emptiness that was inside themselves and they were taking that emptiness for fullness.*

I wondered without hope what divine force or power might remain anywhere in the world that, in the little time remaining before the elevator came to a stop, could hold me back from murdering every one of them in cold blood.

8

1

The End Is Near

He was a student and lived in a third-floor walk-up on Charlotte Street near Chestnut. The tiny apartment consisted of just a room and a half, not counting the bathroom, that being almost too small to turn around in. The larger room (the smaller one offered space just for a bed and side table) boasted two windows, both looking over the avenue. The student spent most of his time in this apartment, since he did his reading there and almost all of his writing as well. Now and then, he did go downstairs and walk along Chestnut to the coffee shop named "Give Me Liberty." The café was desirable in part because you could sit either indoors or outdoors, a nice thing in fair weather. Whenever he went there, he carried a book with him, and always his laptop as well.

But the coffee shop was an added expense, and so he worked mainly at home. Much as he enjoyed the coffee shop, he was careful in budgeting his money so as to have enough for the dinners—or suppers, rather—that he shared every night with Karla, and on rare occasions with one or two others, at their table by the front window at Rosalie's Downtown Café.

A fourth-year graduate student, he had finished all his coursework and had also passed his three required language proficiencies. Left now was only to read for his dissertation, write it, then defend it. He had been at this project for more than a year. He was still reading but had begun some parts of the writing.

His age was twenty-six. College was already a fading memory, five years in the past. His plan was to have his doctorate in hand by spring of 2022, a year and a handful of months from now. What he would do after the degree, he had no idea whatsoever.

•

There was almost no furniture in the apartment: A bed, easy chair, two straight chairs, a kitchen table. He used the table both for a desk and for eating the light daytime meals that he didn't go out for. He had placed it carefully in front of one of the windows so that sitting there he could look out across Charlotte Street. The view was neither rustic, quaint, nor bucolic. In the background, stands of large trees hid grand old houses—as he knew from the walks he took now and then—built back in the 1920s and 1930s. Nearer his own building, however, and closer to his window, was a large empty lot grown up in tuffets of high grass and patches of ungainly weeds. In the very center of the lot, looking rather forlorn, stood a large billboard, held upright by long wooden braces angled behind it.

Instead of facing straight forward, the billboard was positioned at a forty-five-degree angle to the front of the lot so that people driving by would have a clearer—and longer-lasting—view and be able more easily to read the words that appeared on it.

The billboard was never without a message, and that message—although the student had never seen this happen—was changed more or less regularly every three months. Possibly this change was made in the dark of night, or in the small hours of the morning, a fact that would help explain why the student had never seen it actually taking place. In any case, with each season, appearing in the same immense font of black against a pure white background, a different message would appear. For three years he had watched the messages change, and in the third year—this year—he decided to keep a record, recording the messages in his journal.

In July of 2020, the billboard said:

CHRIST DIED FOR US

In October, with a curious ambiguity, it said:

THIS IS A GOOD SIGN

In January, it said:

FEAR, BUT BE NOT DECEIVED

•

He was Robert Carlyle by name, born and raised in Queens, New York. For most of his life, he had been outstanding in academics. After middle school he went to The Bronx High School of Science, and from there to the University of Pennsylvania. Throughout his education, instructors and others in academics found him an unusually sensitive young man, hard-working, conscientious, diligent, deeply thoughtful, and indefatigably serious although not without a sense of humor.

Traits of this kind helped make it understandable that he so ambitiously chose political philosophy and world history as twin fields for his graduate study.

At the same time, however gifted he may actually have

been, he remained relatively private in regard to his own traits and abilities, a habit that was also true in regard to his views about the world. This impulse toward privacy—except with a small handful of close friends, and of course also with Karla herself—arose neither from vanity nor pride, and certainly not from any sense of his own superiority. The truth is that by temperament he tended toward modesty and even toward what most people would consider reticence. This quality of reserve, however, was by no means expressed in postures of archness, smugness, condescension, or superiority. The truth is that by nature he tended toward shyness and even (a life-time habit) toward self-effacement. In school, he had always waited to be called on by an instructor rather than giving the least sign that he knew an answer. In gatherings even now, he was not one to press forward but instead chose to linger near the back, and in auditoriums, movie houses, lecture halls, or classrooms, he chose to sit in the rear, preferably on an aisle.

At the same time, he was neither anti-social nor in any real way stand-offish, as could be seen by his small but close-knit group of friends. It was simply, if you will, that he would rather observe and analyze a race (real or metaphorical) than participate in it. In spite of shyness, he was in fact affable and made friends easily—though only with those who, like himself, were more observers than competitors, more listeners than speakers, more prone to the appeal and value of thought than to the stridencies of argument.

He was inward, but his inwardness was of a generous and giving kind. It lacked defensive walls, and it waited patiently for like-minded others.

•

Two more things need to be said pertaining to his intellectual life.

One is that he did not believe—and since he'd reached

maturity never *had* believed—in even half of what he read.

The other, a thing of even greater importance, is that he did believe, could not help but believe, that everything, *anything*, could be thought by human beings, and that this *thinking* about things was invariably capable of bringing them about.

He had never mentioned this second thought to anyone, not even Karla. It seemed to him one of the most frightening ideas in the world.

·

One day in early March 2021, the message on the billboard changed again. It now read:

THE END IS NEAR: ALL WILL DIE

Gazing out the window, Robert thought about this new message for a considerable time. He went on thinking about it. In fact, he went on and on.

He was accustomed to doing a lot of his thinking in this way, in a kind of abstract reasoning without pen and paper, or, in more contemporary terms, without keyboard and screen. In his undergraduate years at Penn, he had chosen a double major, studying Western history on the one hand and mathematics on the other, the mathematics focusing on topology and non-Euclidean geometry. Partly as a result of his studies in mathematics, this way of thinking an idea through before writing anything down was familiar to him, even habitual.

On the floor beside his table stood two piles of books, each eight or ten volumes high. One was made up of books he had finished reading, while the other consisted of volumes waiting their turn. Sticking out from between the pages of certain of those that he had read, like growths of mushrooms, were slips of colored paper he had inserted wherever a passage or section had especially drawn his attention.

He picked up the top volume from the pile of "read" books and placed it on the table to the left of his keyboard. He opened it to a certain passage, then laid it spine-down. He made sure it would stay open by placing an unopened can of beer on its verso side and a stapler on its recto.

Then he began typing one of the passages he had marked earlier. This one made reference indirectly to the events that emerged in March 2020 and that had had to do with the world-wide programs of propaganda and deceit that were aimed at co-opting and corrupting institutions—institutions of government, medicine, education, journalism, law, the arts—in order to effect massive population reduction by means of medical murder:

> The ever-increasing darkness that has descended like a plague on humanity and is compelling us to race toward our own self-destruction is hard to face, let alone fathom. The evil of our times has become so gigantic that it has virtually outstripped our ability to symbolize it; it has become autonomous, unpresentable, beyond comprehension, and practically unspeakable.

After typing the passage, he inserted a footnote into his text. The footnote appeared on his screen at the bottom of the page and read like this:

[1] Paul Levy, *Undreaming Wetiko: Breaking the Spell of the Nightmare Mind-Virus* (Inner Traditions, 2023), p. 165.

This was his method for beginning a piece of writing. As he made his way through a book or other source, he marked relevant passages with the colored slips of paper. He then later typed out these passages so that, if he chose, he could incorporate them into the shape and flow of his own argument. In a particular chapter of the Paul Levy volume, for example, ("Catching the Bug of Synchronicity"), he placed a veritable crowd of "post-its" in order to identify five closely-related passages that he knew he would want to refer to later in his own paper. The first of these passages was this:

In Buddhism, this principle of intercausality (a third type of causality) is called dependent co-arising (also known as interdependent co-origination) and it is considered the fundamental dynamic by which empirical reality is continually reconstituted in each and every moment. Basically, this principle says that everything is interconnected. Everything affects everything else. Everything that is, is because other things are. What is happening now is part of what happened before, and is part of what will happen next. (p. 267)

"People in general" [Robert typed, combining his own words and some of the author's words, with the aim of providing a transition] "believe 'the very convincing appearance' that time has duration and that it therefore is 'unfolding in a linear, sequential way' with one moment following another. 'This gives birth to the [incorrect] notion of a linear sequence of distinct moments that arise one after the other, like a conveyor belt.'"

He followed this transition by typing out the second passage in full:

Emerging out of this [incorrect and wrong] way of looking at things is our illusory conception of linear sequential time, which as quantum physics has pointed out is nothing other than a construct(ion)—a creation—of our mind. In fact, based on our experience, we always find ourselves in the one and the same singular, unchanging "now" moment, which is a realization that can't help but transform the very consciousness that has realized this. (pp. 267–268)

"This unity and oneness," [Robert typed, this time in his own words] "is a unity and oneness not only of time but also of space."

And then:

An expression of the interconnectedness, interdependence, and undivided wholeness of the universe, where there is no separate self to be found and no separate things of any sort, dependent co-arising operates throughout space at any given moment in time as well as in each moment. (p. 268)

[Once again, in a combination of his own words and the author's words, Robert typed:] "The apocalyptic calamity has been glacial in its pace and also as unstoppable as a glacier, until it has become, now, 'practically unspeakable.' *The reasons for it are clear, the escape from it less so.*"

Then he continued, typing this passage:

The tragic and unnecessary confinement of our minds to a linear-sequential logic can be seen as a reflection of what has happened to much of humanity in its fall into the overly rationalistic scientific materialist paradigm. Although grant-ing humanity immense power over the physical universe, our entrainment in scientific materialism has sadly atrophied our immensely powerful inner psychic and spiritual faculties, changing many of us into misshapen, one-sided, unbalanced creatures. (pp. 268–269)

And finally:

The compensation for the one-sidedness of humanity as a whole must come through the reawakening of these atrophied and dormant inner faculties of the mind. (p. 269)

•

It was now nearing the third week of March, and the air, although not yet dramatically warmer than before, carried a scent and texture that hinted at the approach of spring. For as long as he could remember, when people asked his favorite season, Robert had always answered that his choice was autumn. Now, however, he had changed his mind. If he were asked now, he would choose spring, without question.

It was a quarter of six. He had walked along Chestnut to Merchant and at number 538 gone up the stairs and rung the bell for apartment 3-B. He was now waiting on the front porch for Karla to come down. The building she lived in dated from the early 1920s. Three floors high, it had been constructed as a boarding house for summer visitors, but now, a century later, it was given over to rental apartments. The tenants were mainly students, like Karla, who rented by the semester, although there was also a generous sprinkling of retirees, who rented for the long term.

The front porch extended across the breadth of the house. Like the porches of many other houses in town, it had, long ago, sported rows of rocking chairs for renters to use on their long summer evenings of "taking the air." Now, however, the porch was entirely empty of chairs and looked curiously vacant. Robert leaned against one of its white-painted columns and gazed out over the quiet street. His mind was still grazing over his day's reading, and he thought to himself: *1) This moment is now; 2) all moments are this moment; 3) this moment is all moments.* And then: *1) This place is here; 2) all places are this place; 3) this place is all places.*

Then he thought, remembering the billboard:

THE END IS NEAR: ALL WILL DIE

He took in a deep breath of the early spring air. There was a sweetness to it. It carried with it a scent of moistened earth.

He waited for Karla. She would be down soon. Together, they would walk over to Rosalie's Café, four blocks away, on Langdon Street. Together at Rosalie's, they would have something to eat, and a beer, maybe two, near the front window, at the table they liked.

And they would do the same the next night. And again the night after that.

They would, of course.

He was quite certain.

About Atmosphere Press

Founded in 2015, Atmosphere Press was built on the principles of Honesty, Transparency, Professionalism, Kindness, and Making Your Book Awesome. As an ethical and author-friendly hybrid press, we stay true to that founding mission today.

If you're a reader, enter our giveaway for a free book here:

SCAN TO ENTER
BOOK GIVEAWAY

If you're a writer, submit your manuscript for consideration here:

SCAN TO SUBMIT
MANUSCRIPT

And always feel free to visit Atmosphere Press and our authors online at atmospherepress.com. See you there soon!

About the Author

Born in 1941 in Northfield, Minnesota, **ERIC LARSEN** graduated from Carleton College in 1963 and took his doctorate from the University of Iowa in 1970. For over three decades he taught in the English Department at John Jay College of Criminal Justice, retiring in 2006. His debut novel, *An American Memory*, appeared in 1988, winning the Chicago Tribune's first Heartland Prize, and was followed by *I Am Zoë Handke* (1992); *The End of the 19th Century* (2011); *The Decline and Fall of the American Nation* (2013); and *The Book of Reading* (2023), completing a five-part saga of family and nation. Larsen married the late Anne Larsen, editor of *Kirkus Reviews*, and the couple raised two daughters, Flynn and Gavin, both now active and highly productive in the arts. Larsen lives in New York City and is author also of the non-fiction works *Homer Whole: A Reading of the Iliad* (2009); *A Nation Gone Blind: America in an Age of Simplification and Deceit* (2006); and *The Skull of Yorick: The Emptiness of American Thinking at a Time of Grave Peril—Studies in the cover-up of 9/11* (2011). His website is www.ericlarsen.info.